SEEDLINGS

SEEDLINGS
STORIES OF RELATIONSHIPS

ETHEL LEE-MILLER

To Hank, who is always with me

CONTENTS

SEEDS

SHOOTS

BLOSSOMS

Epilogue

ACKNOWLEDGMENTS

People and places have been so central to these stories that I had to make a list. Readers who know me are surely not surprised at this—I get pure contentment from making lists. This list is certainly one that brings contentment and gratitude.

My sister, Eileen—my womb mate, conscience, and joy.

Paul Benson—for the pure pleasure of knowing you.

My parents, Allan and Gladys Erickson—their imprint on my life is etched more deeply each year.

Cousin Al Blunt, Candy, Sue S., Kay Ball, Marcia Dobler Levine, Ann Chapman, Jeannie Gerdy, Majda Fisher, Catherine Garland-Hicks, Rose Cole, Grace De La Forterie—for sharing seeds, stories, and lots of laughter.

Samantha Chetta Carroll and Charley Collier—for the memory captured in a photo.

Groundwork Promotions—Stephanie and Paul, I can't begin to add up the hours of support.

National Stroke Association

New Jersey inspiration—The Write Group of Montclair; Adler Aphasia Center; Washington School—West Caldwell.

Tucson, Arizona havens—Sunset Writers, Roadrunners Toastmasters #3850, Starbucks, Caffe Luce, the Redemptorist Renewal Center—for providing a venue for people to come together for education, support, or food for the body and soul.

INTRODUCTION

Seedlings: Stories of Relationships

I may not have a green thumb in the garden, but I have an incredible number of seedlings. My seedlings are the stories, essays, and poems that have grown out of overheard conversations, things that happened to me, milestones, dilemmas, and celebrations of friends and family, even a quick verbal snapshot from a scene at Safeway.

My seedling stories are all from various gardens of relationships, the majority coming from seasoned, mature gardens. *Seedlings* is divided into three sections: Seeds, Shoots, and Blossoms. The seeds stories grew from an aha moment, an overheard word, or a germ of an idea. The shoots are family, friendship, and marriage stories that came with some plot, some background, and beginnings, and maybe a flower or two of an ending. Several of the blossom stories were delivered complete to me directly from the garden of someone's life. A "Genesis" or "Garden" statement either introduces or concludes each story.

Just as my sister's daylilies need to be cared for—to be watered, fertilized, cut back, and admired before they are given away, my words have been planted, watered by me, culled and cut back, and enriched by feedback from my writing colleagues before they have been gathered into this bouquet of stories for you, the reader.

Enjoy!

1

SEEDS

The seed stories are short snippets told over lunch or at a family gathering that I immediately thought could be expanded to reveal some aspect of relationships. Seeds are best germinated to create seedlings by wrapping them in a moist paper towel, or in a seed tray indoors. I've wrapped the seed essays with a setting, characters, dialogue, and a theme. All have been watered and nurtured with "what ifs," "maybe this is what happened next," "perhaps this is what happened before," or "I wonder ..."

Some seed stories came from one-word reminders or quick scribbles on restaurant receipts, clever lines I heard and jotted in my writer's pad that I keep with me at all times, anecdotes told at meetings and saved on the notes page on my phone, and articles torn out of magazines and newspapers. All with the thought, *This would make a great story!*

THE SEVEN-SECOND
CONNECTION

The Handshake was something my dad taught my sisters and me, not by saying "Watch and learn" but just by being himself. This got me thinking of those thousands of things parents and other adults teach us in similar ways.

As an oversensitive eight-year-old, I could be embarrassed by my father in about seven seconds. It wasn't that he was obnoxious or unattractive. Even as a child, I saw that my father turned heads with his straight posture, his twinkling gray eyes, and a certain openness that made him so appealing.

It was precisely that easy friendliness that made me cringe. As shy young girls, my twin sister and I had learned to create our own world and often didn't need anyone else. Was it because Dad wasn't a twin that he needed to greet every passing soul? Everyone in church already knew him. Did he have to be on this campaign to get to know everyone in the suburbs of New York?

"Hi, I'm Al Erickson," he'd say to anyone, with a hand out for a warm handshake. "This is my wife, Gladys, and my girls, Ingrid and the twins, Eileen and Ethel," and he'd go down the line introducing us. All with a big smile on his face.

"Put out your hand. Four fingers together. Thumb up a little. Firm. Strong," he would instruct us for The Handshake. Every Saturday during the summer, we walked to the post office in a small town out on the north shore of Long Island that was our haven in the summer. As soon as the person next to us had clicked their P.O. Box closed, Dad was ready. He'd stick out his hand for the greeting. We all learned to follow suit. Smile and shake.

It never occurred to me to explore the why of my preadolescent discomfort. I just knew he was like that everywhere—at the corner store, at the library, even on the street.

"Jeez, Dad, we don't even know them."

"Now you do. You may be the only person who says hello to them all day."

As I got older my perspective on the world shifted. I noticed the reactions to his handshake. Strangers were sometimes slow to shake hands, but they did. The hello was often just an opener. When Dad shifted his weight and brought both hands up to make a point, I knew we were set to "jaw awhile."

I learned how to make friends all with a quick handshake and a smile. The boundaries of my father's world were marked by the towns in which he lived. But I believe he was one of the best goodwill ambassadors around. And he had fun doing it.

As I got older, the routine came naturally for me. It gave me a way to mask my own shyness. As a teacher in New Jersey, I made a commitment to personally greet each child within the first ten minutes of class. In professional groups greeting nervous new members or guests, I still hear echoes of "You may be the only person who says hello."

Imagine my sigh of relief in 1997 when I stepped into a room full of strangers and a man named Mike Quinn, I'll never forget his name, stretched out his hand to shake mine and gently pulled me across the threshold into Wayne Toastmasters. By the time I began my second career as a counselor and life skills presenter, The Handshake was my own. Sure, I'd get nervous before I spoke to a group. *I don't know anyone... What if...* But after about two minutes I'd realize a truism I've used for almost twenty years was at work—we are more alike than different.

In 2007 I was ecstatic to have my first book published. *Thinking of Miller Place: A Memoir of Summer Comfort* has lots of twin stories and, yep, the story of Dad and The Handshake is definitely in it. I spent a full year doing book signings and talking about the power of words—both written and spoken. And I had fun doing it.

In 2009 my husband and I moved from New Jersey to Tucson. On our neighborhood walk, a "good morning" was often the seven-second connection with a new friend. Going to first meetings of a writing group, Toastmasters, a yoga class, the "what ifs" still start chanting in my ear. But when I get to the door, a handshake and smile pull me across the threshold. Hey, I know how to do this. Thanks, Dad. I'm home.

The Garden's Harvest: Rather than let the "what ifs" stop me from going somewhere new, I take The Handshake along with me wherever I go. Rather than feel old when I have the good fortune to meet young folks from Generation X or Y, I relish the comparisons and the look of amazement when we find common ground. It's always true—we are more alike than different.

NOT MY TRIBE

I never gave much thought to the age of people who hovered around the periphery of my life. As time goes by, the periphery is pretty full, and I find I actually look at them. Is it a product of being a writer and noting my surroundings for sensory tidbits? Or is it something about, dare I say it, aging?

Now that Borders has gone the way of other overexpanded chain stores, where are all the fifteen-year-olds? The Borders employees behind the checkout counters and stocking shelves, or self-consciously wearing the plastic badge of Manager, were a microcosm of young people, as my dad would call them, experimenting with hair, clothing, and body adornment styles.

They were a population lifted out of a high school early apprentice program. The young males appeared to be about fifteen. The females looked an in-your-face twenty-one, but the insecure body language of a sixteen-year-old betrayed them. Didn't they know they were beautiful by virtue of their smooth skin and shiny lustrous hair (although sometimes a lustrous pink or blue) and young bodies that could smoothly lift themselves from a crouched position at the bottom bookshelf to a standing position in an effortless three seconds?

The young men caught my attention. Green hair and body piercings covered all natural signs that they were chronologically eighteen, twenty-one, or even the ripe old age of twenty-five, but they were physically and socially stuck in tenth grade. My Borders Music Department when I lived in New Jersey consisted of one very pale, plaid flannel-shirted, jeans and Keds-wearing youngster. He was impossibly thin with veined hands that a sculptor would love. He flipped through CDs as I hummed the first two lines of yet another song whose title eluded me. My eyes were drawn to his long neck and the whorls of blond hair that skewed to the left side. His youth took me back to the days when Jefferson Airplane was not an oldie.

And yet there was much to admire in the adolescent cornucopia of information and resilience in this camouflaged sector of society. He always called me "ma'am." Music Department Manager and his cronies put up with parents using the children's section as daycare. They were inordinately neutral and calm in the face of outraged customers whose expired coupons could not be accepted—or else these employees could function quite well while stoned. Although they did not have that cheery smile that the Starbucks baristas have, they always made somewhat indifferent eye contact.

Some of these fifteen-year-old lookalikes yearned for the active life. Walking that thin line between juvenile delinquency and law-abiding citizen, they chose legal gun carrying and became police officers.

Heading home one late afternoon, I admit to exceeding the speed limit. But I had already reached my limit as an elementary teacher that day. A class of twenty-five second-graders had stolen all my patience. A below-freezing February day in New Jersey meant no outside recess for fear the little childlings would freeze. I just wanted to get home.

Of course, it was a no-brainer that I eased through the now-turning red light at the left turn signal. The red flashing light atop the Eagle Fells police car right behind me revealed yet another reformed delinquent patrolling our highways in a bubble-top car. Pulling over and reaching in my purse for my license and registration, I glanced in the side mirror. I could see by his frame and walk that my officer of the day was one of the very young lads of the EFPD. Thank God he worked in Eagle Fells where the biggest crime was probably a resident smashing his own window when he was locked out.

"Evening, ma'am. License and registration." As I handed it over, I filled in the age checklist. *Peach fuzz. Check. Smooth skin. Check. A whiff of Irish Spring. Check.*

"You know you went through a red light there, ma'am."

"Yes."

I saw his hands shifting the license to the top of my documents. "Well, I'm going to have to . . ."

I looked up. My officer of the law was turning a bright red as a flush traveled up his neck and across his cheeks.

He leaned down and looked me in the eye. He handed the cards back to me. "Here you go. I can't give you a ticket, Mrs. M. You were my second-grade teacher."

Who knew my career choice would bring that kind of diplomatic immunity? My senior citizen companions and I are on the lookout for more of these creatures.

Another place they seem to thrive is on local morning talk shows. I have a friend who was interviewed by a man and woman whose collective age appeared to be below thirty and who spoke in sentences reminiscent of the Dick and Jane books.

My friend Bruce arrived at his mother's house to see a fire truck parked outside and two "youngsters" on their cell phones. As he ran by, they reassured him, "False alarm, sir." His mother had called the rescue squad when palpitations and dizziness gave her a scare. The fifteen-year-old in charge took his mother's blood pressure and talked gently to her as he held her prescription bottle in his hand.

"Ya gotta take this blood pressure med when it says, Mrs. L. See here?"

Bruce had gone through this conversation more than once with his mother, who had impatiently brushed him off. But his mother listened to the man-child because of the blue shirt and logo that said "Paramedic," which equaled "Authority" in her mind. Yet she has a sixteen-year-old grandchild whom she proclaims is a ninny.

You will never see the fifteen-year-old clones in some places. Country club grillrooms and spas, that's a given. Gray-haired people inevitably drive flashy little convertibles, usually a metallic silver or dark green. Attendants at fast-food drive-through windows now have a median age of about fifty-two.

The fifteen-year-olds have migrated to Tucson, where my husband and I have retired. I think my New Jersey Borders advisor is now a manager at Best Buy. His companions have moved to Apple.

Take Eric, he of the little-boy haircut but serious and respectful manner of a well-trained geek. Eric, my Apple genius, doesn't understand women like me who grew up being told, "Don't touch that switch." He is in unfamiliar territory when he advises, speaking quickly, as they are wont to do.

"Just play around with your iPod/iPhone/iMac."

My eyes take on the deer-in-the-headlights look, and my fingers hesitate over the keyboard. My digits have not been brought up to play around with things. They need steps one, two, and three. Stop. Wait for instruction. A look of "puhleeze" flashes across his face when he sees this roadblock to techie advancement. Then it quickly vanishes. He loves computers and so will make nice to the middle-aged and senior folks who come in droves each day for lessons, advice, and to contribute to the Apple coffers. He is, after all, only fifteen, and he has all the time in the world.

A New Romance at Forty

Too much of a good thing is wonderful. —Mae West

Ya gotta learn to laugh; it's the way to true love. —John Travolta in *Michael*

If lots more of us loved each other, we'd solve lots more problems. And then the world would be a gasser. —Louis Armstrong

My life has been filled with many varied experiences—meeting people, teaching, coaching, traveling, dancing, trying new foods, writing, public speaking, cultural events, reading… The list goes on. I view life as a glass half full, and I want more. I'm a pretty upbeat person, yet can feel "the lows" acutely.

My first marriage was a happy one. Granted I was young and went into it with very romantic ideas. My husband and I had challenges—financially, culturally (a racially mixed marriage), professionally, geographically (I worked in New Jersey, he in New York City), and emotionally (did I mention I was young?).

But we were committed to our love and met each challenge head-on. We both believed in the vow of "for better or for worse… 'Til death do us part." And tragically that is how our marriage ended. My husband died. After his traumatic death, I swore off marriage and emotional dependence. Through years of grieving and "growing up," I learned how to take care of myself, to be solitary, and not lonely.

Eventually I yearned to be in a true committed relationship again, and I had a pretty good idea what that meant.

Just when I was reconciled to being *single... for... the... rest... of ... my... life*, I met Hank.

Well, first I heard his voice. I was at a meeting and heard this deep composed voice from the back of the meeting room. I was stunned. Not only did the voice sound good, the words that were spoken made sense. When we met face to face, I was almost besotted.

For weeks after I met Hank, I was like a schoolgirl. How could that be for a woman nestled right up next to the age of forty? Believe me, it happened. When Hank asked me for my phone number, I hoped he could read it because I felt so shaky being near him. I recognized the signs of infatuation—lust, preoccupation during work hours, boundless energy, losing weight, clear skin, strong sense of well-being.

By the time Hank and I decided we were in love, we knew we were also in like. We got to know each other—talking, meeting my family, meeting his daughters, walking, going to plays, and avoiding sex for ninety days. Ah, that one caught your attention. Can you imagine? A woman who came of age in the 1960s carrying around a piece of paper with her that said "No sex for ninety days." That was an interesting conversation. One in which I also had a glimmer that this was a solid relationship.

Over a romantic lunch with Hank in an outdoor café in New Hope, Pennsylvania, I shared that the "no sex for ninety days" was a suggestion for a healthy relationship for people who often put the cart before the horse, so to speak.

There was a silence. He looked at me. *This could go either way.* I knew I was willing to have the romance end if he could not go along with this. He cleared his throat and spoke. "Well, this is not what I want right now, but if you need to do this, okay."

I exhaled. This would work.

We saw each other as much as possible. We took walks holding hands. We kissed, hugged. We talked. He phoned me each day. We had long dinners. He sent flowers. I wrote him little love notes. I smiled and laughed. I was like Maria in *West Side Story*. I could do no wrong; he could do no wrong.

One evening Hank and I were talking about love, about being together for the rest of our lives. In other words, commitment.

"Well, we could move in together," I suggested.

"But that's not commitment," came that deep wonderful voice.

"What do you mean?" I went into full debate mode. "Cathy and Jack have been together for decades. And look at René and Rob. They just bought that house together."

"No," came the firm voice again. "The next time I make a commitment, it's with marriage and in front of my family, friends, and God." He looked directly at me.

This little gem of an idea squeezed down into my heart, made its way through years of old fear and vulnerability, and I literally squeaked, "Oh, Hank, if that could only happen."

We were engaged in April 1989 and married in October 1989. We wrote our own ceremony that included affirming each other as individuals, and affirming our love to each other. We read our ceremony before our family, friends, and God. Having God in on the deal sealed it for me.

Couples and family therapy was where Hank and I got *the* pearl of wisdom. We were told simply that we (the husband and wife) were the primary relationship. This was, and has been, a rock to lean on when we were unsure of where to begin in any kind of struggle.

The keystone of our relationship is "Be the architect of your new relationship, not the victim of an old one."

We have had twenty-four years of a deepening marriage. Love, respect, caring, and laughter seem to surround us. We read our marriage vows at each anniversary. Our home is a haven for us, our friends, and an open door to his family, my family, and our family.

There is no question that problems arise. We use what we know to work them out. When we don't know, we go to meetings, read books, talk with each other, attend workshops, talk with trusted friends, and again, talk with each other. Life is not a hardship for me in this marriage; we rarely fight. We talk. I can frequently wait to have these talks "tomorrow after dinner," because I know between this morning and dinner tomorrow he is not going to throw all his clothes in the car, storm out the door, and drive out of my life.

We are the primary relationship.

Our counselor gave us those five words: "You are the primary relationship." But it was after we had used them and I found myself telling other couples the strength of those words, I knew I had to write this part of our love story. Because it's true, and because I'm on a mission to combat the thinking that:

» *There are no good men/women out there.*
» *You have to "settle" if you want to be in a relationship.*
» *You are lucky if you are happily married even once.*
» *All of the above.*

THE LOVE SEAT

This seed was planted after I complimented my dear friend Majda on her wicker furniture collection. We always get or learn something, not always material, from a relationship.

On their first date
He took her on the two-hour drive up the New York Thruway
To the quaint town of Rhinebeck,
Because she loved old furniture—
And Rhinebeck boasted antique shoppes, cubbies, and hidey-
    holes of wood, metal, estate sale, and wicker treasures.

She fell in love with the wicker love seat.
He bought it for her and strapped it on the top of his 1979 VW.
They drove home singing "Islands in the Stream," the love seat a
    wicker crown on the roof of his car.

The seat found a home on her screened-in wraparound porch.

They added a wicker hanging chair, rocker, and lounge,

A plant stand for the deciduous Long Beech ferns and five ceramic
candleholders.

Delicate lily of the valley scented the porch when the twilight
breeze blew

Off the lake while they made love on their Rhinebeck beginning.

She didn't stay with the guy, but he started her on the wicker collection.

THEY WERE IN LOVE
AKA DYSFUNCTION JUNCTION

Sometimes you have to go through the torment of finding out what you don't want in a relationship in order to know what you do want.

It was the perfect relationship.

He had the apartment—

She had the car.

In a fit of anger, she threw her stereo out the window—

He gave her his.

He wrecked his car—

She bought him a new one.

They were in love.

Windows of Opportunity

 Emotions have been the seeds for stories. When my father died, I was struck by the image of the nurses gathered around his doorway and the stark simplicity of two tears. When my mother died, I wrote this piece. I revised it when my dear friend Mary Ellen died. When my brother-in-law died, I pulled it out and read it for comfort. Can you see how this passion for writing is called a process?

The activity, serenity, and pure happiness of our married life has been marred the last two years by the deaths of four dear friends and family members who were also our peers. Groping my way through the grief, I came back again and then again to the truth of death being an arc that is part of the circle of life.

Intellectually, this sounds really mature and solid. Emotionally, I am uneasy and squirm even as I write this. It brings back the memory, as has happened before, of the year my father died. Then I breathe again as I go through the memory.

It was late afternoon by the time we pulled into the circular driveway. I could see my mother's silhouette framed in her kitchen

19

window. It wasn't until we walked into the kitchen that I saw her face. There was no smile, no frown, devoid of emotion.

"He's gone. They just called," she said. "Your dad died ten minutes after you left the nursing home."

It had seemed only by chance we stopped to visit my father at the nursing home before ending our journey at my parents' retirement home thirty miles farther on Interstate 26 near the Blue Ridge Mountains. Some people might call this one of those windows of opportunity.

Two days before that, my husband and I had been packed and ready to drive west to Dayton, Ohio, for his annual family reunion. When my mother called with the news that my father had been in and out of consciousness, the choice was obvious to us. Drive south to Carolina instead of west to Ohio. A choice easily made without conscious thought. A choice wrapped in years of family interactions, laughter, tears, arguments, hugs, and lots of sustaining love.

The first day driving south, the cell phone kept us in touch with my mother. The second day was alternately stormy or misty and consistently gray. Near Route 40, in Carolina, a terrible curtain of black smoke and then flames spiraled up on the road ahead. An accident closed Route 40 in both directions. The detour was bumper to bumper.

My theory of car travel is forward motion—always forward motion, even if it means zigzagging to keep moving. The traffic spill-off from the accident was at a standstill.

"Get off here," I said as we approached an unmarked exit. A window of opportunity. My husband turned onto a rural road that wound its way through small towns toward Interstate 26. We passed a sign that read Hendersonville.

"We're closer to the nursing home than Mom's. Let's visit Dad first then go down to Mom's."

The nursing home hallways seemed unusually bright and sunny, muting the aroma of cleaning sprays, urine, and sickness. A group of nurse's aides clustered outside a room, their pink flowered jackets making an oversized bouquet by the door. Stopping to look at them, I read the nametag on the wall—Allan Erickson. My father.

I had just seen Dad three weeks earlier. We knew he was dying. Years of cancer and Parkinson's had captured his movements and robbed him of physical strength and vitality.

"Wait, this is a mistake." The man in the bed was so tiny. His eyes were closed; he was so still. That couldn't be my father. Only a slight movement under his shirt told us his beating heart still held his spirit here.

"He hasn't opened his eyes since yesterday," his nurse said.

I took his cool curled-up hand. All my life, my father's strong, warm, square hands had been a part of my growing up—holding on to them walking on the boardwalk on Long Island so I wouldn't feel afraid, watching them briskly flick the thick bristled brush back and forth over our Sunday shoes—"so you can see your face reflected in 'em"—watching entranced as his hands fashioned kites out of scrap wood from his basement workbench. Carpenter's hands, we called them.

"Dad, it's Ethel and Hank. We came to say good-bye." This frail man's eyes opened and stared straight at me. Parkinson's had frozen his facial muscles. He had no voice, but his eyes stared, gray and cloudy, at me.

My kiss left a funny lipstick smear on his cool, yet perspiring, forehead. "I love you, Dad. We're here now. It's okay now. We're all together." I moved closer to sit on the white-sheeted bed. "We'll take care of Mom. You can go."

As I shifted my weight on the edge of the bed, his eyes still stared straight ahead, but no longer at me. I moved back into that straight line of sight. *Could he see me? Could he hear me?*

"I have a song for you, Dad. Remember this one? 'You are my sunshine, my only sunshine...'" I sang the family theme song of childhood car trips.

"You've helped me so many times in my life. I'm so grateful to you.

Remember when you told me the best thing you could do was let me grow up and take care of myself? That was so true.

"Remember all your friends? You helped them. You helped me. Now I help people. And it goes on and on."

Could he hear? His eyes stared straight ahead but two tears formed and slowly slid down his cheeks.

So we said good-bye.

Windows of opportunity. Do we create them, fall through them, or receive them as a gift?

The choice to drive south instead of west was ours. But this created a window of opportunity.

The choice to visit Dad before Mom, a window created—by what? Some Higher Power?

I've had windows of opportunity open to me almost every day. I've probably missed lots of them. It's my choice to decide if I use that window.

With each loss of parents and friends from my life, I renew my promise to create one window by making a conscious choice to say "I care" or "I love you" to someone even though it seems they can't hear or acknowledge me.

If it's my friend's baby who can only gaze back at me. He hears me.

If it's my neighbor's teenager torn by those first sharp attempts at independence. She hears me.

If it's my sister, "chosen" sister, or spouse, and all I see is their back turned to me in anger. They hear me.

If it's my aging parent moving beyond my physical grasp... He heard me. I know he did. I was blessed with those two tears.

Ankle Bracelets and High Tops

One image after another gave me the theme for "Ankle Bracelets." Pure visual candy.

My new hometown of Tucson offers a wide spectrum of types of homes, outdoor activities, lifestyles, and choice of dress.

I am fascinated by the broad array of ways people adorn their bodies. It's not like I haven't seen a wide variety of dress styles—hey, I lived in New York City, although that was in the 1970s. This is different. Tucsonans embrace a Southwest cowboy/independent/orneriness, and, on rare occasions, a weather-influenced choice of clothing.

When I lived in New York, the TV weather channel's local report included a small inset with graphics of what clothes to wear—jacket, sweater, boots, scarf, coat, hat, or gloves, all meteorologically advising us, "Don't leave home without it." Such advice would be scoffed at, ignored, or more truthfully, not even noticed here in Tucson. Regardless of age, Tucsonans dress with abandon, or care, and march to their own sartorial drumbeat.

Recently my husband captured my attention when he arrived home after his gym workout. He had on his usual retirement ensemble of shorts, T-shirt, sneakers, and the ugly gray sweatshirt jacket that I have unsuccessfully tried to get rid of. But what drew my eye downward was the blue-and-brown argyle socks. Knowing I still hold on to remnants of strict style consciousness, he had his reply ready. "I wore these socks earlier today and thought, 'Why dirty another pair?' I'm saving laundry."

Not long ago, a woman with incredibly thick, long silver hair, greeted me in line at the post office with, "Jeez, it's freezing," as she briskly rubbed her black-and-white polka dot gloves together, protecting her sun-worn hands. That she also had on white cut-offs seemed not to enter into the picture.

What kind of thinking drives Tucsonans in their dress habits? Not for them the categories of classic, preppy, professional, casual, bohemian, or Goth.

Take today. Here I am at one of the ubiquitous Starbucks, land of laptops and caffeine, amid the din of clattering silverware, and offers of at least ten kinds of coffee mugs in eight different colors. The seating area is one tiny space with four lounge chairs, eight very small square tables, and two double-size tables—highly coveted and always occupied by a single caffeine drinker. The outdoor seating is twice the size but minimally occupied today since the temperature has dropped to fifty-eight degrees. There is a total cloud cover, and I actually had to turn on the windshield wipers on my way here. Despite my New York weather origins, I agree with the natives. It's downright chilly.

Most sojourners are wearing long pants. When the temperature dropped this morning from seventy-five to sixty-nine degrees, I changed from jeans and sandals to tights and my Uggs, and actually threw on a poncho. On line at the cashier, I meet a middle-aged gentleman wearing shorts and white sneakers with his upper torso protected by a T-shirt and windbreaker, and a mustachioed four-sugar coffee enhancer donned in baggy black shorts, sandals, and a fleece jacket with arm emblem proclaiming World Sculler Champion.

A young, exceedingly tall beauty wears running shorts and a snug sleeveless red top with nary a goose bump marring her physical appeal.

A leather-jacketed drinker is seated next to a skinny camisole.

A tall, bearded, very thin man hurriedly left his laptop and post at the comfy leather chair, dashed out the door, and reentered less than ninety seconds later pulling on a tan overcoat before hunkering down once again over his laptop.

A latte drinker wears black pants, flats, and a sweater jacket over a T-shirt that proclaims, "My therapist eats kibbles." She also has on tiny Chihuahua earrings.

Amidst the independent fashion statements is one traditionalist—a button-down white- with-blue pinstriped shirt wearer with a navy blue tie, black dress pants, and very polished black shoes.

And on this chilly day in Tucson there is only one hat wearer—a mustachioed gentleman of a certain age wearing a gray baseball cap that says in white capital letters "TUCSON."

EMPTY NEST

I was only going to write about the hummingbirds coming and going, and I realized our house is our nest. Going back in time, I thought of other "nests."

Empty nest. Always sounded sad to me. Those two words evoked memories of the little hummingbird nest we had observed last spring as Mama Hummer built a tiny home near our back patio for three equally tiny eggs.

Each morning I tiptoed up to the nest, which was precariously placed between a cluster of leaves and the place where the leaf stems met in a V at the branch. Why did she build so near the edge?

Then one day the eggs were gone and in their place were three little squirmy things. They were, I'm sorry to say, quite ugly. But Mama H. evidently thought otherwise because she flew off several times a day and came back with nourishment for her darlings. For several weeks I used my weak-powered opera glasses to get an update on the babies. They finally started to resemble birds, twisting their little heads in darting movements as Mama hovered overhead with the meal of the day.

The triplets got bigger and switched positions in the nest.

The next development was when the fledglings started lining up on the edge of the nest. Just sitting there? Or were they literally getting the lay of the land, scoping out a future flying pattern? I spent an inordinate amount of time staring out the window, either waiting to see them fly away or being at the ready to rescue them if they flapped their miniscule wings and took a nosedive to the stone patio.

And then one morning they were gone. Babies gone. Mama gone. Maybe they were out on a flying lesson? All day I was drawn back to the nest to look for the family. Gone.

Soon after Hank and I got married, we began planning to get a home of our own. I had moved into his house with his two teenage daughters, now officially my stepdaughters, and I, their stepmother. Correlating closely with our motto of being the architects of our own relationship, not copying the blueprint of another, we decided we needed a new home. Not his house, not my house, but our house. A home for our blended family.

We drew up plans for what we needed: space, amenities, and convenient location to work for Hank, the girls, and me. Two older teenage daughters at home would need a degree of independence within the physical setup of our new home. Our current residence had the bedrooms and bathrooms but no separate area for socializing other than the living room, which was open to everyone who entered the house. Maybe a split-level home. Definitely needed several bedrooms and bathrooms. Three women and one man in a house. Think about it.

My summer vacation task was to look for a house that met our criteria. Somewhere in the course of looking at the fifty houses that made the first cut, our daughters made the decision to get an apartment on their own. I was pleased about this.

Before I sound like the wicked stepmother, let me share my belief. I defined grown-up as out of school, out of your family home, living on your own. This meant an apartment shared with a girlfriend, boyfriend, or as a married couple. Only rarely did first-apartment dwellers have the luxury of living alone. My first apartment in 1969 was a really small nest halfway between where I worked in New Jersey and the college from which I had recently graduated on Staten Island. The five-hundred-square-foot studio apartment offered privacy and independence, but no extra space. I was so proud of being able to live on my own.

Contrast this with Hank's family's belief that girls lived at home until they got married. I remember being truly surprised when my one stepdaughter shared that she thought she would live with her dad until she got married.

Hank and I were in agreement that we wanted "the girls," as we called our daughters, to stay with us as long as they felt it necessary along with preparing them to live on their own. Sort of a blending of my idea of grown-up and his. Just having them get a place of their own without preparing them would be like the baby hummers taking a flyer out of the nest before they were ready. We talked budget and decorating and saving for our new home as a way of prepping them for their first apartment. We started having them get ready to leave the nest. What did it cost to buy food, clothing, and necessities? Just what came under the category of necessities?

But at the same time, I kept looking at large homes with walkout levels and a huge garage for four cars for four adults.

When the girls told us they were going to find an apartment together, I was surprised but felt they were ready. We set up insurance and AAA to take care of a certain kind of security. I regret that I did not spend more time at their new apartment, but I felt they wanted to be independent. I didn't think then that I was letting them slide out of our daily lives. Now I am not so sure.

And so it seemed as if one day they were gone. Not far physically, but far in that we were not at home every evening in case they needed us. Gone. Empty nest. Did they feel an emptiness too?

We ended up buying a condo ten miles from our daughters. Hank had an easier commute into New York City. I had a nine-mile commute to work in West Caldwell, New Jersey. We were proud of the painting and decorating the girls did in their new home and that they seemed excited to be "on their own." On their own, but only a few miles from our home. I hope they felt some security in knowing their nest was near ours. I know I felt a kind of invisible protectorate knowing we were still close to them, just in case.

The year after the hummingbirds nested in the tree by our back patio, I felt a frisson of excitement one morning as I went out to the driveway to get the paper and saw a blob on the edge of a branch in the front oak tree. Moving closer, I saw it was a tiny nest. So small it could only be a hummingbird nest. Not the same tree, but a nest near ours.

CRAGGY

The seed for this essay was a single word in a magazine article. Craggy. It's a catchy word—has a good solid sound. But the connotations got the seed growing.

I've always liked Harrison Ford, from his early days as the dashing Hans Solo to the nearly superhuman Indiana Jones. Forty-five years ago he earned a $125 paycheck for a few lines in *Dead Heat on a Merry-Go-Round*. It just got bigger and better. *Star Wars*, *The Fugitive*, *Air Force One*, *Patriot Games*, *Raiders of the Lost Ark*, and *Cowboys and Aliens* in 2011. He's been triumphant in each decade.

I am reminded of a *Parade* magazine article in 2012 about Harrison that resonated with me. "Harrison Ford, at 67, is guarded, quiet, and thoughtful. His face is handsome and craggy, and his eyes are kind." A perfect description of what one might look for on Match.com. And yet, I am bothered by one word. *Craggy*. Especially when combined with handsome.

My dictionary tells me craggy is an adjective meaning rugged, rocky, and steep. No connection with my irritation. My female hackles rise. Could it be something gender and age related? He is five years my senior. He's craggy and handsome. This gnaws at me. *Craggy*. I research further. My thesaurus leads me from craggy to rocky, then to lined. Aha, now we're getting somewhere. An example, "His visage is lined with those fine lines that mark his life experiences." Well, so is

mine, but no one has equated my fine lines with physical attraction. They are sometimes weakly labeled "laugh lines."

A recent blurb touts Mr. Ford's chiseled features as the next possible model for Mt. Rushmore, of all things. Apparently he is a man who can be utterly comfortable in his own skin, craggy though it is.

"Am I craggy?" I ask my husband in what I admit is attempted in a hopeful, beguiling manner. He looks straight at the TV. He knows this could be a tension-ridden situation. Which tack shall he take? Honesty? Humor? Feigned hearing impairment? He does his Rex Harrison imitation. "Why can't a woman be more like a man?"

"No," I protest. "I don't think that's it. I don't want to be like a man. I just want equal rights being craggy."

Random googling leads me to similar uses of cragginess. My sad findings: Craggy looks are accompanied by a gravelly, but authoritative, voice and tanned and/or work-worn hands of the male gender. These descriptions, ever since the days of Shane, Cheyenne, and Richard Boone in *Have Gun, Will Travel*, link cragginess to solitary toughness and an ethical character.

I go back to my tried and true resource tool. I google "actresses over sixty." Tina Turner, Susan Sarandon, Helen Mirren. They are described as "awesome, elusive, *still* enchanting, adventurous." Somewhat linked to character but no physical attraction connection. Craggy is not an equal-opportunity adjective.

My husband leans over my shoulder. "Remember those excerpts you read to me from *Men Are from Mars*? Men and women are different," he intones as he goes off to bed.

More frantic googling. Female celebs. Hillary Clinton, Madeline Albright, Diane Sawyer, Martha Stewart: "Savvy, intelligent, icons." But no crags.

I find an archaic meaning of crag. A sharp, detached fragment of rock.

Is this what people think of craggy women? Are we sharp and detached? *Crag* also comes from the Scottish meaning neck or throat. A nasty image.

Since there seems to be no way women will change society's opinion on this subject, the thing to do is turn it into a money-maker. I'm sharing this with my readers. I can run off thousands of copies of this piece, preferably done in very large font, to every plastic surgeon and doctor who does Botox, face peels, and facelifts. I'll have it laminated and placed on tables in waiting rooms. Headline: "Women Say No Crags for Us." Every woman who comes in for a consult will sign up for every possible procedure ASAP. I will ask for but a small commission for each one. I'll end up with more laugh lines, but someone else will pay to get rid of them.

I do one final google for craggy tidbits to use in my PR pitch. An older Internet entry lays out Prince Philip's description of Edmund Hillary: "A very human, very unassuming, but obviously a very tough, craggy character." Again, craggy associated with very human traits but also very male.

I shut my laptop and retreat to bed. My husband is engaged in some deep snoring but stirs as I arrange and rearrange the blankets around me.

"Have you given up on the craggy thing?" he mutters.

I sigh, which is neither defeat nor defiance. It's only a regrouping device until tomorrow.

I move closer to my mate. In the glow of our nightlight, I peer at my husband. He's getting some fine "laugh lines."

His muffled voice comes from the depths of his pillow. "Stop looking at me. Go to sleep."

Of course, he's okay with all this. He's aging the same as I am. But the difference is he's becoming ... well, craggy.

Things I Love About
My Body

My dear friend and writing colleague, Ann Chapman, was the muse for this when she shared her affirmation list of what she loves about her body.

Spring is coming—warmer weather, warmer sunshine each day, outdoor fun! And yet I see headlines like these:

4 Steps to Whiter Teeth!
6 Brain Foods You Need Now!
8 Ways to Improve Intimacy!
10 Exercises to Be Bathing Suit Slim!
12 Tummy Trimmer Ideas for Spring!
14 Foods that Give You Shinier/Sleeker/Shorter/Longer/Thicker Hair!

Aargh! What's the message in all this? *You are not good enough the way you are.*

I can't go through my supermarket checkout without magazine headlines telling me to shape up! Or... turn to the other side of the checkout and give in to my junk food addictions.

Here's my weapon against this checkout line onslaught:

Eleven Things I Love About My Body

1. My head—it has a great shape, it readily holds my eyes, nose, and mouth, which I have opportunities to use each day.

2. My mind—which is constantly humming with ideas, messages, realizations, turning feelings into thoughts, messaging muscles into action.

3. My teeth—which lovingly crush, chew, and gnash fruits, vegetables, *and* chocolate chip cookies to sustain me.

4. My smile—which opens friendship doors every day.

5. My skin—which is smooth and sensitive to tickles and kisses.

6. My eyes—which are dark brown, showing me incredible views of people, nature, and the new books on sale at Barnes & Noble.

7. My hands—that can button clothing, pat my sister's shoulder, caress my husband's face, and hold my grandnephew.

8. My arms—which are long enough to reach for the lightbulb in the closet and strong enough to be an anchor for my aging friend.

9. My hips—which are useful for things both sensual and functional, like swaying and nudging the car door shut.

10. My stomach—which is soft, slightly round, and is my daily food processor.

11. My feet—all size eight-and-a-half of 'em, which faithfully walk, run, and dance me through the day.

What are your eleven?

A seed for you: Come on—everybody reads those headlines at the checkout counter. Got writer's block? Go buy one item at the grocery store just to walk through the magazine headline maze. What do you love about your body? Think of all the possibilities for stories.

COMPASSION AMBASSADORS

Have you ever seen Angel Cards? Small cards with positive intention words. There is one word on each little card with a colorful illustration of a tiny angel. My husband and I choose a card at random each morning. The seed—I kept picking compassion, and at a time when my patience was pretty thin, stress level was high, and personal vulnerability was obvious. Coincidental? I was also rereading books by the authors mentioned in this story. I volunteered to give a speech on compassion. This story had to come next.

I admit to being a self-help junkie. I buy the books, read online blogs and websites, go to workshops, and listen intently with pen poised to take notes when someone tells me they've had some kind of breakthrough with an emotional problem or relationship.

I know a lot about the way things ought to be, or what I ought to say to empathize with and support people. But sometimes it's hard. *Do you hear the bit of a whine in my voice?* Take being compassionate. I find myself thinking, *I really want to be compassionate, but now is not a good time.*

Compassion, so Pema Chodron and Jack Kornfield tell me, is the ability to understand the emotional state of another person or one's self. Empathy is the ability to put myself in another person's place. True compassion goes to a deeper level. It means I can feel and might want to actually reduce the suffering of someone else.

What gets me stuck is... me. I get stuck in what I have found out is the storyline of a situation.

Pema Chodron, a Buddhist nun and teacher, talks about the storyline as going ahead of an action with a "what if" thought. If I think people are just being mean, I am unwilling to reach out to support them. *What if she rejects me or gets angry?* If I use scarcity thinking in my decisions, I use "attic generosity." Ouch, that one hits the target. I can recall numerous times I've held on to dishware, clothing, even old costume jewelry that I had not used for years in kind of a greedy hoarding. *What if I need it sometime? Better just put it in a box in the attic.*

Storylines contain pre-existing propensities, things ingrained in us. For example, Jane is a horrible neighbor. She always complains about kids making noise. She claims the odor from our barbequed steaks invades her house, and she's not even a vegetarian. Rob is charming. He always notices when the ladies in the neighborhood have gotten their hair done. Of course, he's also a hair stylist so the first place he looks is at our heads. These are the storylines that influence my interactions with Jane and Rob.

So who will I feel more comfortable helping, Horrid Jane or Charming Rob? Duh. But when my solid ground is upset, I am upset. I find out Horrid Jane has cancer and is suffering. I know I will take a casserole over, or offer to drive her to chemo, but first I need to work through my propensities. Being compassionate asks me to begin to get comfortable with not being on solid ground. Tough stuff.

I am in training to stay in the present, to interrupt my old habitual propensities and reactions. I hear my former yoga teacher suggesting in her low confident voice, "Allow old judgments to rise and pass by as if on a radar screen...And then let them go." I am assured that by doing this my suffering will lessen. Yes, yes, I want to lessen my suffering; I don't want to feel irritated when I am around someone who is, shall we say, difficult. Sometimes the radar screen image works, other times I follow the complaint/judgment blip around and around. This all makes sense when I read it, but I admit to stubborn resistance in the actual use of the premise. Who will be my role model to help me with my resistance? Instantly a memory from my teaching career comes to mind.

A fifth-grader is taking a crying kindergartener to the nurse. She puts out her hand and the crier lifts hers up without hesitation. "Come on, we'll go to Mrs. E. She'll fix it."

"Is she the one who always lets you pick the color of your Band-Aid and calls you sweetie?"

"That's the one."

"Okay. That will be good."

And off they go. Safe and cared for.

Aha. My role models have been in my life for years. Let me respond to situations like a well-loved child who reacts from innocence and caring and being in a place in the world that is safe. Young children don't have old habitual thoughts. They don't have old storylines. They're not old.

I think young children are the most compassionate of people. In my teaching career, I watched over two thousand kids walk, run, stumble, and skip into my classroom. I've seen and heard laughter, anger, frustration, enthusiasm, depression, hurt, and compassion. I could pick out the budding compassionates in the first few days of school. The kid who deliberately lagged behind to help the shy one put on his backpack. The child who shared her Fig Newtons with the classmate who had mere plain crackers for a snack.

I sense more verification might be necessary. One year I had a really ultra-bright child in my second-grade class. He usually shouted out answers as soon as a question was out of my mouth. Yet he chose to sit next to our newly arrived and silent student from Zaire. Ornella was quite tall for a second-grader, with large dark eyes, clutching her spiral notebook and brand-new pink backpack. She arrived without any knowledge of English and spent her first days in school sitting at her desk and shaking her head, "no no no." First Smarty-pants did the "me, Tarzan, you, Jane" greeting until they got their names straight. Then he started drawing pictures next to words in her notebook and leaning over and saying, "door, door" as he pointed to the classroom door then the closet door. Then, sliding his hand under the word he had written, he said "dooooor" slowly as I did when I read aloud to the kids from the chalkboard. *Wow, he's been paying attention.*

I've seen kids nurse each other. Putting on Band-Aids or rubbing the hurt elbow. I've seen them coach each other, literally running parallel with a classmate who just never got the gist of getting from one base to the next in kickball. "This way, Tim, this way!"

The class prankster even had his moment of compassion with the kid who was the Different One. Really. That was his nickname. You know, the child who never knew to run when there was trouble and so got caught.

I overheard a planning session for a forbidden but tempting experiment. Our classroom was on the second floor, and there was a large window out in the hall that in today's school would most likely be locked and barred. The window slid open easily and just begged to be part of a physics experiment testing gravity and velocity. The deal was for one kid to slide the window open so other kids could toss their backpacks out as they left school at the end of the day. They all would race down the stairs to see whose went the farthest.

Instructions to the Different One were more explicit than simply "toss and race." Prankster yanked Different One over to the window as they came in from recess. "Meet us at this side window when the dismissal bell rings. When we throw our backpacks out the window, throw yours out too."

And here, Prankster pulled out his tough-guy persona. He got right up in Different One's face. "You are allowed to take only *one very fast look* out the window to see where yours lands, and then you *have* to run down the stairs really quick 'cause Ms. G. will be out in two seconds. Remember last time when you were watching all the packs go down and Ms. G. grabbed you? Remember? You had to stay after and you hadn't even thrown yours out? So today, toss and run. Got it?"

Different One probably didn't know the what or why of the exercise, but he did know he was being included. He was positively beaming as he heaved his backpack out the window, papers flying, and his brand-new if-you-lose-these-you're-dead glasses sailing jaggedly behind his unzipped bag.

One of my most touching experiences with compassion came as a result of my own sadness. A teaching colleague had died, and I was explaining to my second-graders that there would be a substitute for me that afternoon when I went to the funeral.

"Are you sick?"

"No, I am not sick, but I feel very sad about Ms. D. and I want to go with my friends to kind of say good-bye to her. I have a funny lump in my throat, but it's not from a cold."

"Are you coming back?"

"I will be back in school tomorrow. But today I need to do this."

Some of the unsolicited pearls I got from my seven- and eight-year-old compassion practitioners were:

"Sit with Ms. Gerdy so you can hold her hand if you are sad and need to cry."

"When the church is over, go out and stand in the sun."

"You have to feel sad for a while. It will take Ms. D.'s soul a few days to get to heaven, and then you will not be sad anymore."

And finally, "Here, you can have my tissues. I only used a few of them."

Intuitively, these openhearted children knew compassion called for human contact, being one with nature, acknowledging feelings, and sharing.

Feeling sad? Here, sit by me. I'll hold your hand and share my tissues.

From the Garden: Thank you, Jeannie Gerdy, for the years of teaching, laughing, and learning together at Washington School.

AGING—IT'S ALL RELATIVE

My friend Sue and I always asked each other, "How's your family doing?" Both our mothers were in residential homes. Both were feisty, aging, and winning a pretty big place in our hearts. When I shared about my mom's birthday, it prompted her reply.

Sue was celebrating her great good luck at being a first-time grandmother of baby Gerald John.

The entire family had gathered to celebrate the birth and to honor the grandmother and a great-grandmother. Four generations of women were represented along with adult brothers and sisters.

Sue's ninety-two-year-old mother-in-law was delighted with her new great-grandson. In talking to her son, the talk turned to ages. Her conversation suggested she thought she was talking with a much younger son.

"How old do you think I am, Mom?" he asked.

"Twenty-seven?"

"No, Mom, I'm fifty-six now. Andy is fifty-nine, and Patty is sixty-two."

With a shocked expression on her face, she replied, "Oh no!" Then, as an ever-protective mother, she leaned over to him. "Please, don't tell them!"

Losing Things

Everyone loses things. Sometimes smaller items: pens, sunglasses, socks. Sometimes valuable belongings: a bracelet, a credit card, a ring.

But for the last few years I've been losing more vital items. Soon after I turned fifty-five, the daily scrutiny in the bathroom mirror revealed a loss here and there. My hair lost the shine of youth. Easily fixed with a deepening relationship with my hair stylist. My skin began to lose elasticity and firmness. More hours in the gym, using crèmes, and wearing Spanx helped.

Rather than be shocked by these visual losses, I turned to my bellwether for aging. My twin. My twin sister and I are separated in age by a mere five minutes, but this carries some hefty weight in the trip down the aging path.

Developmentally, things happened to her first. She walked first. She grew taller first. And the same has been true in other more mature aspects of aging. So she gives me a heads-up on the aging process.

I remember when she called me up to announce her first gray hair. I cluck-clucked and tsk-tsked in sympathy and raced to the mirror as soon as I got off the phone. Front of hairline, part, sides. No gray. Yet.

Some months later she called again with the latest report, a change in eyebrow shape, color, and texture. "Texture?"

"Yes," she said. "One lone eyebrow hair is growing longer and is actually coarse and sticks up on its own."

"But…but, that's only for grandpas who are really old and geezerly."

"Not true."

Sure enough. I soon had one unruly eyebrow hair over my left eye just like my twin. Some years later we commiserated over the permanent lessening of eyebrows in general, but not the coarse one. It could stand on its own—sort of like the cheese in "The Farmer in the Dell."

Recently my hairdresser hummed a bit during my latest cut and blow dry. "Hmm. Your hair is getting thinner on this one side."

Now, I had accepted that my hairline had decreased up along the sides, no more tightly pulled ponytails for me. But overall thinning?

"No!" I exclaimed.

"Yes," she affirmed. Another loss remedied with some camouflaging gel and a bit of pouffing in the styling.

Next aging report. "So here's a quirky one," Twin related. "Get ready. When I was blow-drying my hair I noticed I have some hairs that bend."

Bend? We have broom-straight hair, which has made me nurse a twinge of resentment that my father did not share the wavy hair from his side of the family.

I heard my twin's intake of breath, the wind-up for the full telling of the bending hair situation. "As much as I tried to curl it under, it kept popping up at an odd angle. But I found a solution. More gel and a product called Mudd—a texturizer and thickener."

I got used to these physical maturing reports. There was a certain amount of security in knowing my sister was just a bit ahead of me along the road of aging.

Until my sixty-fifth birthday. Where was I going that required the use of the magnifying mirror to apply lipstick? Must have been a bit special, because this called for a darker color as a foundation under my everyday gloss. When I stepped back to look in the regular mirror, my upper lip was totally uneven, even though I had followed the lip line. My upper lip was just a thin slash across, dipping into almost nothing from the fulcrum out to the right corner. I was appalled. Could it be I was losing my upper lip?

Perhaps my vision was going? The only handy consultant was my husband.

"Does my lip look funny?" I asked my sweetheart. Wrong time to ask. Hank was at the computer, which meant his body was in a locked position, eyes staring straight ahead, right hand frozen on the mouse.

"You look fine."

"No, really, look." I should have known this was fruitless. He was ready to go out and so was engrossed in the latest CNN online news while he waited for me. I resorted to the old tried-and-true method honed by Scarlett O'Hara over a literary century ago. *I'll think about it tomorrow.*

Next day I did a scrupulous facial check in the magnifying mirror. Straight on, smile, tilted head angle, smile. I checked for signs of a stroke—smile, wrinkle nose, and stick out tongue. I passed those tests, but that upper lip was definitely disappearing. I called my twin.

"Are you by any chance losing your upper lip?"

"Supper dip?"

I guess hearing is going too.

"No, upper lip. I am losing my upper lip. It's thinner. It's crooked."

"Hold on. Let me see … No, I'm okay. Maybe you slept funny."

It's amazing the rationalization that can go on when vanity is involved.

"I don't think so."

My womb mate is not as sympathetic as I would wish. "I gotta go. I'll call you later."

This leaves me alone and abandoned with the phone heavy in my hand and my disappearing upper lip.

Ensuing weeks had me poring over beauty catalogues and online sites to address this problem. My peers in my writing group all seemed to have their upper lip intact. These were women who have shared about hysterectomies and implants, both dental and other.

And yet I just couldn't bring up the subject of my disappearing upper lip. When I tentatively broached the subject in my book group, two women nodded knowingly, and another nodded *and* shrugged in acceptance. I have set up the acceptor as my role model. She is usually calm and in good humor at every monthly meeting. I'm working up the courage to ask her what she does about the mirrors in her home. In the meantime, I have given up darker lipstick for pale lip gloss and more dramatic eye makeup.

The disappearing upper lip influenced me to build up my verbal repartee rather than just smile during conversations. I have since learned to live with its disappearance. It's okay, really it is. Especially since I noticed other folks are experiencing losses too.

My husband was pouring a coffee refill at the kitchen counter and I noticed his pants were kind of sagging in the back. I went to give him an affectionate pat and felt empty material.

"Good heavens, you're losing your butt!"

"Yeah," he said. "That diet is working."

I felt the need to be joined in my upper-lip loss. "No, maybe it's an aging thing."

Hank turned to face me. He was feeling sassy. "Well, at least I'm not losing my upper lip." And he kissed me you know where.

The Seed Revealed: The lost upper lip did it. It forced me to reluctantly look back at aging things that have happened. Since it could be a depressing retrospective, I decided to use humor and take my twin along for the ride, as she has been every step of the way.

SHOOTS

Shoots generally refer to the new, fresh plant growth. They include stems but also can include leaves or flowers. Shoots are supported by tender roots and a strong stem with the nodes holding a few buds. The shoots essays and relationship stories have been embellished by me with descriptions and details and watered to full bloom. Some shoots are character sketches that served as a relationship connection for me. Some are watered with a bit of exaggeration. Some are hybrids making a composite character from two relationships meeting in a new context or in a different time and place.

Take a walk along the garden path of my shoots.

A Summer Portrait

I could have had no better adult idol than the character in this story. The idolization led me to watch her every move and remember each detail of her clothes, her walk, her grace, and her charm. So it was easy to write the full character sketch. All I had to do was think of Chanel.

My idols for beauty in the summer of 1958 were the Breck Shampoo girl, the Miss Rheingold girls, and my precious movie star paper dolls. The neighborhood teenage beauty, Starr, was my real-life idol. But the epitome of adult beauty in my eleven-year-old life was wrapped up in a living icon known as Mrs. Desmaisons.

Suzanne Desmaisons vacationed each summer in a small pristine cottage up the hill from the beach. Where our summer house was big and open with bare floors, her wooden floors were covered by little throw rugs. That always made my twin sister, Eileen, and me laugh. How could anyone imagine throwing rugs at Mrs. Desmaisons's house?

Plain white sheers bordered our pane glass windows. Crisp curtains with tiny paisley designs embraced her windows. Her gardens had little iron benches alongside, and the pathways were layered with tiny white pebbles. We didn't run along her pathways. We walked as slowly and gracefully as we imagined a princess would.

In the cluster of moms who dressed in bright print bathing suits and short terrycloth cover-ups, Mrs. Desmaisons shone like a mature polished jewel. Most summer mothers wore Woolworth sunglasses and colorless lip balm at the beach. Mrs. Desmaisons wore red lipstick—at the beach, and had brilliantly blue eyelids protected by sunglasses that had little sparkly jewels at the outer edges. Her short silver hair was tucked neatly under a turban as she sat under a small beach umbrella in her solid dark red, one-piece bathing suit. It seemed she had every color suit, from vivid red to chic black, pale yellow, even pink. Her nails were oval-shaped and smoothly color-coordinated with the suit of the day.

Mrs. Desmaisons was my introduction to Bain de Soleil and Chanel N°5 Parfum.

Suzanne Desmaisons was French. She established my lifelong romance with the glamour of Paris, France, in fact, anything French.

Mrs. Desmaisons's daily entrance on the beach was a premier walk-on. She paused at the top of the ramp on the hill, bringing one hand to shade her eyes under the brim of her straw sunhat.

Although not more than five-feet-five inches, she held herself so straight she seemed tall. Her walk added credence to the practice of walking with a book on your head for good posture.

When she began her regal descent, the fringe from her black gossamer beach poncho rippled around her like small subjects surrounding their queen. She would glide down the ramp with some young, or not so young, admirer carrying her wooden picnic basket, beach chair, towel, and sun umbrella.

She herself carried her straw beach tote over one arm. Her low beach chair was placed on her SD monogrammed beach towel like a throne. After sitting, she carefully emptied her beach bag—a book, jeweled reading glasses, thermos, and suntan oil gently laid out on the separate small towel next to her beach towel. She always sat at a slight angle to the water. I would replicate this scene many times at the beach as an adult.

Mrs. Desmaisons was like other summer women in that she

stayed in her house alone during the week, while her husband, Louis, pronounced "Lou-ieee," appeared from some fascinating profession and accompanied her to the beach on weekends.

"I bet he's a diplomat at the UN," Eileen whispered.

"Or a clothing designer," I added, thinking of the ideas he would have for my cutout dolls.

"Maybe he's even the owner of Chanel!" breathed our friend Honey.

"Ah, Lou-ieee." Mrs. Desmaisons would smile at him from her throne.

"Ma Suzanne," he would say, gazing at her, eyes crinkling at the corners with delight.

"Suzanne. Lou-iee." My twin whispered their treasured first names as if to say them any louder would break the spell of glamour that drifted around Mrs. Desmaisons.

The only similarity with other summer moms was the absent husband. Our little country village was populated by women and children during the week, while the husbands and fathers who worked in "the city" drove out each Friday evening for a short weekend respite before the Sunday evening trek back along congested highways to their home.

Mrs. Desmaisons was at least ten years older than the other moms, yet seemed ageless. Their only child, Louis Jr., was called "Young Lou-ieee" and was not as young as we. He was old enough to drive.

At least once during the week, Young Louis would be seen waving from the top of the sand dunes and then moving gracefully down the ramp to the beach. Where everyone else thumped or ran down, Louis Jr. moved deliberately and lightly, almost on the balls of his feet. He would always greet us as he moved by our clump of kid beach blankets. "'Allo, ladies."

In my mind I envisioned my hair swirling in slow motion away from my face across my shoulder as I smiled shyly, yet with a hint of boldness, in silent reply. In actuality, he probably was greeted with three openmouthed, gawking girls as he went by.

His mother remained seated as he bent over to give her not one, but two kisses, one on each cheek. *How did they know which cheek to do first?* When my twin sister and I tried it, she always turned into my mouth and we ended up bumping jaws.

Mrs. Desmaisons was a mermaid at the water's edge. Her swim began by slowly wading from the shoreline in up to her knees. She would dip one hand in the water and bring it to the opposite shoulder and down her arm, acclimating limb by limb to the water's temperature. First left arm, then right. We watched entranced.

"Will that be all today or will she swim?" Honey asked.

Honey, Eileen, and I turned on our beach towels to watch and learn.

If it was to be a swim day, she waded in farther, up to her chest, and then, leaning to her right side, she slid into the water.

"Okay, there she goes. She's going in."

Cupping her right hand in the water and pushing with the left arm, slowly exhaling with each push, and a slight flutter kick, she was launched like a graceful new canoe out from the shoreline. It was from Mrs. Desmaisons I learned of the breaststroke. Eileen, Honey, and I spent many hours perfecting the Mrs. Desmaisons Swim.

"'Allo, watch me!"

She swam left to right from our beach buoy to the boundary of the public beach, and then back. Then she slowly swam in, rose out of the water like a water nymph, and walked in a meandering kind of way back to her towel.

The post-water part of her swim consisted of carefully drying her arms and legs, patting her face dry, then sitting, and…drying her feet. Then the reapplication of lipstick, with lips open, then pressed together as she tilted her head to view her face in a tiny round mirror.

By then we had drifted over toward her towel on our way to re-enact the swim, catching a flutter of her heaven-scent Bain de Soleil.

"Hi, Mrs. Desmaisons."

"Hi, Mrs. Desmaisons."

"Hi, Mrs. Desmaisons."

She paused with jeweled sunglasses in hand, so we got a full glance of those flashing eyes. "'Allo, mes petites."

This greeting dissolved us into a mass of girlish arms clasping each other as we staggered under the weight of such a loving hello.

We turned back by the shore to get one final look. Leaning back and stretching her arms overhead marked the last act of her swim performance. As she slowly lowered her arms, her contented sigh coincided perfectly with the moment her fingers touched down on the sand at her sides.

Aaah!

BIG AL

Cousin Al told us the anecdote about "those childproof locks" at a family gathering one Christmas. I knew I had to write something about his laugh and generosity that only seemed to expand as he aged. This story hit the spot.

Cousin Alfred was always a big man. When I was eight, an impressionable preteen, he was in his early twenties, a six-foot-three Air Force flier with a booming laugh, ready smile, and a hug for everyone.

I always looked up to him. He was a flashy dresser, very cool and handsome, with glamorous girlfriends at a time when I was quite curious about this boyfriend/girlfriend thing.

Al loved to eat. He used to say, "I always sat next to your dad at family parties; he was a big eater too." At Thanksgiving dinners his plate *was* the cornucopia several times over.

When he approached his seventies, Al had mellowed but was still a big man. Think of an NFL linebacker who hasn't worked out for thirty years but tends to chow down like the big game is tomorrow.

He wore khaki pants, Hush Puppies shoes, and plaid shirts, never tucked in, with the front rising slightly higher than the sides and back, as most of his bulk was in his stomach. So picture this: big man with the big smile, big hug, and big laugh.

A big man like that needs a big car. When the other grown-ups were talking about boring things like cooking or rebuilding the backyard shed, he took my sister and me for rides in his cars. In the 1960s, it was the biggest American-made sedan with the longest fins. In the 1970s, it was a red convertible.

In the late 1980s, Al went to South Fork Chevy and got himself a sea-green Chevy Caprice Classic, the largest sedan they made. It is described as " ... a behemoth, competent ... for buyers who need interior acreage, lots of chrome, and miss the good old horsepower-infused days of the '60s and '70s ... A car popular in police and taxi fleets, which carries plenty of passengers and cargo."

Just the car for Cousin Al!

As he drove it the eight miles from the dealership to home, he noticed the windows and chrome were a bit smudgy. "I'll fix that as soon as I get home."

Pulling into the trailer residence around 10:00 that morning, he was like a soldier returning home. The neighbors always turned out for Al's first ride home in his new cars. He'd lived at the trailer park for twenty years. So had most of them. He traded up in trailers as regularly as he traded up in cars. Always the best, always the biggest.

After the crowd had touched, honked, readjusted the mirrors, and drifted away, Al got out the Windex and paper towels and went to work. Even though it was a big car, it wouldn't take long. He knew the new-car routine.

When he stepped back to admire the job, he noticed a smudge on the inside of the back window. "I'll just reach in and wipe that." Not an easy task for a close to three-hundred-pounder. But he managed to get to it by sliding on one leg along the backseat with the other leg sort of hanging out the side door, Hush Puppy keeping that door open.

While he was cleaning, Bill Holland went by in his Chevy on his way to work at Grumman. Al couldn't help but feel a bit smug as he waved to Bill. Here he was living the good life, sprucing up his new Chevy, as Bill went off to work with the other drones.

As he stretched to get the final swipe, he had to scooch over just a bit and pulled his leg in for balance. And the Chevy Caprice Classic behemoth door slowly, but heavily, swung shut.

Now in seventy years, Al had gone through many life experiences but had deliberately missed three. One was getting married. A second was having children. The third was reading instructional manuals. "Never had to read one yet," he proudly proclaimed after he told us Pauline Newton was the one who came over and hooked up his VCR.

So of course it never occurred to him that there would be a negative consequence of this particular literary miss. When he went to get out, the back doors were locked. He was a seventy-year-old victim of childproof locks.

He tried in vain to reach across the headrest to get at the on/off switch to disengage the child lock on the back door. He was big, but his arms were disproportionately short, a fact he had never noticed until that awkward moment.

Helen and Jim Muller drove by on their way to late breakfast at the Sunrise Diner. Tuesday was short stack special. They waved in response to Al's frantic gestures and gave him the thumbs-up signal.

But Al was a survivor. He threw all logical measurement of mass and space to the winds and lunged forward between the seats and headrests to get at the switch or front door handle. And he became lodged from the armpits down between the seats.

Al was not given to using expletives, but he did call various Biblical characters into his life situations. "Holy Moses. *Oh* my God. Oh *my* God. Oh my *God.*"

It wasn't either of them who came to the rescue but Dorothy Wilkerson, with whom he had had a torrid affair a decade ago, who sauntered across the lawn to check out the new car.

"Dorrie! Dorrie! Dorrie!"

"What in heaven's name are you doing hung in between those seats, Allie?"

"I'm stuck, that's what."

"Oh, just open the door," she said and pulled open the back door

by Al's right foot, letting in a much welcome blast of air along with her signature scent, overdose of Tabu.

"It's the new childproof lock. I didn't know it was on."

"No problem," she said. "You just got to flip this doohickey here inside the door. My son has this on his car."

She sat on the seat, pushing Al's foot in even more. "There now, I think it's off."

And she pulled the door shut to test it. Dorrie was not a manual reader either, and her observations regarding her son's car were not correct. So there they were. The both of them. Dorrie stuck under and behind Al's sit-me-down so she couldn't reach forward either.

They had some time to reminisce about the old days where Dorrie told Al, yet again, why their relationship had waned due to his fear of intimacy and over-possessiveness with the TV remote. Al was only glad that he didn't have to see those veins at the side of her neck that always stuck out when she got worked up, and that she was forced to direct her lecture at his southernmost end.

Well, it was Bill Holland who was the savior. When he came home for lunch and saw Al still in the car, *and* with Dorrie, he meandered over to visit.

"Whatcha both doing in there?"

They screamed, "Get us out and don't shut the door."

Al was so grateful to be out of the confines of the backseat and into the open air that he took both Bill and Dorrie for Tuesday short stack special, his treat.

And to prove what a big man he was, he was always the first to laugh whenever anyone asked him how he learned to operate those childproof locks.

EVOLUTION OF A HEALTH NUT

My husband's casual observation about the contents of our refrigerator got me thinking about how much my mother's health philosophy had a positive influence on my own habits, through obedience as a child and by choice as an adult. I made a list of things I learned from her, which became this shoots essay.

Most families in the neighborhood of my childhood greeted the day by setting the radio dial to music or news. At my house we were greeted with the serious, articulate voice of Carlton Fredericks as my mother boiled eggs and sparingly buttered our morning toast. Carlton Fredericks was a food nutrition consultant on WOR-NY long before anyone was counting fat grams or knew their own personal LDL or HDL. In my childhood in the 1950s, my mother was known as a health nut. Carlton and Mom, it was a match made in airwave heaven.

My sisters and I were eating whole wheat bread when it was really *whole* wheat. I knew I'd never be afflicted with scurvy as I thankfully downed huge capsules of vitamin C with my orange juice, not orange drink. We were served large portions of green peas and other dark vegetables before anyone stalked the wild asparagus with Euell Gibbons.

One evening, in a move of subversive childhood revolt, my twin

58

sister and I pushed the peas off our plates and lined them up inside the napkin drawer of the dining room table. My mother's eyes widened in surprise when she saw our empty plates. Usually we lingered at the dinner table long after my parents and older sister had finished. We were of the "children are starving in China" generation and had to clean our plates of all morsels of food. I looked everywhere except at my twin as she slid the napkin drawer shut. I just knew if I looked at her the nervous laughter in my throat would escape and I'd have to confess. We suffered the short-lived guilt of knowing those peas were drying up inside the maple table drawer while my mother nodded approvingly. "Finished, I see," she said. "Now that wasn't so bad, was it?" And she uttered her closing statement, "Vegetables are good for you."

I remember the day I became a sugar addict. I went into Dee's Luncheonette with Tommy Alkin, a well-known neighborhood candy connoisseur. The candy rack was conveniently located smack in front of the cash register where Mrs. Dee chain-smoked Pall Malls and watched for young, quick-fingered candy thieves.

"I like Black Jack gum," Tommy boasted. "But I won't get it today because it makes your tongue black and girls don't like that."

"Oooh," I gushed. I knew the ropes of boy-girl conversation.

"Here, your mother would like these. They're called Chuckles and look like slices of fruit." Everyone knew my mother's dietary leanings.

That was the day I was also introduced to Turkish Taffy. "Just keep pulling," Tommy said as I tried to take a bite-size bite. The pink candy stretched and stretched. The zing of pure sugar bonded with my taste buds and shot right to the pleasure center of my preadolescent brain. I got greedier and greedier, trying to bite and get more in my mouth at the same time. "Oh, take the whole thing," he said. "It only costs five cents."

Hot fudge, whipped cream, and a cherry on top of ice cream never graced the table in our childhood home. We had yellow Jell-O. Not with whipped cream but with lots of grated carrots and a few pineapple chunks. Occasionally the Jell-O was red, if my mother was in a slightly reckless mood. Meatloaf was infused with wheat germ. Chicken was lightly sprinkled with flax. The salt and pepper shakers were placed on the table, always within the protective reach of my mother, to stop excessive sprinkling. She could also hear more than a few shakes even when she was out of sight in the kitchen. "That's enough salt now" let us know the mom surveillance was in working order.

In my teenage years, when my body craved Twinkies, pizza, Tootsie Rolls, and gum, I whined and resisted our home nutrition plan. "This house has no good food in it. Donna's mom buys ice cream for them all the time."

My mother countered with her strongest weapon—fear. "Your good friend next door, Donna, has cavities and will lose all her teeth before she is thirty." Oh, but that couldn't happen because of Turkish Taffy, could it?

However, as I aged, I saw my mother aging and retaining the skin and figure of a woman fifteen years her junior. She swallowed vitamins the size of small birds' eggs with ease. She knew multiple uses for apple cider vinegar. Her face was unlined and her hair was still thick and shiny even as it went from gray to silver.

On my own after college, I bought a few vitamin jars and switched to whole wheat bread or better yet, rice cakes and brown rice. My refrigerator was a nutritional schizophrenic mix of sesame butter and some tofu along with coffee and the soggy doggy bags from Friday night dates.

I frequently called my mom for advice. Migraines: "You're eating chocolate again, aren't you? Take apple cider vinegar." Gall bladder: "Get psyllium husk capsules, open two capsules, and mix in with your orange juice. Drink it right away. Otherwise it will congeal into a mess in the glass."

I was thrilled when she bought me a heavy-duty Acme juicer for my thirty-fifth birthday. My refrigerator welcomed ten-pound bags of whole carrots and celery. I felt positively smug when I got my first *Physician's Desk Reference* and placed it proudly next to Earl

Mindell's *Vitamin Bible*. It occurred to me that I might be surpassing my mother in health, nutrition, and well-being habits. Or at least the knowledge of such habits.

One Christmas my mother gifted each of her adult children *and their husbands* with gaily wrapped packages of flax seed. Not one to take false credit, she attributed her generosity to an error in a catalogue order that got her not five pounds, but fifty pounds of flax.

My husband accepted all of this as long as there was "real food" in the house.

"I've got to have red meat," he proclaimed.

"Well, sure."

"I like potato chips and dip."

"You want junk food," I barked, "you buy it." I was tough. He bought his supply. He was also a softie. He never refused when I found I needed "just a smidge of that Ben and Jerry's Chunky Monkey that you have in your bowl."

One morning as I came down to breakfast, Hank was standing in front of the refrigerator, just staring. Thinking this was the beginning of one of our "Where's the butter?—It's right in front of you" conversations, I probably was a bit defensive.

"Our refrigerator is starting to look like your mother's," he commented.

"No way!" I joined him in the draft of cold air and followed the trail of his pointing finger. Sure enough, there were seven, count 'em, seven Tupperware containers with food products of varying hues of green and brown—the swampy ecru of my leftover cabbage soup, dark green of paper towel–wrapped kale, a container of powder for my daily green drink. Thirteen bottles of vitamins had taken up residence along the shelves of our refrigerator door.

I had become my mother.

My Mother's Hands

Seeing a jar of Pond's Dry Skin Cream in a CVS Pharmacy stimulated the idea of gathering all the different ways I have thought of my mother's hands and the stories that went with them.

I've always been interested in my mother's hands. In childhood I compared the activities of her hands with those of other mothers. Some mothers' hands baked cookies for school birthday celebrations, poured milk into Clarabelle glasses, and knocked gently before entering rooms. Other mothers' hands were bejeweled, held magazines, or got their nails lacquered.

My mother's hands were not put to such use. My mother's hands wrote out grocery lists, smoothed down bedsheets, and wrung out the wet laundry of three daughters and one working husband before efficiently snapping it and hanging it outside to dry. My mother's hands were seldom used for gentle strokes against a child's face, but they did occasionally coax the notes of "Für Elise" from the living room piano.

Her thin white hands moved with rapid little jumps creating shopping lists, reminders, or notes. Geraniums, ivy, and coleus blossomed under her hands that watered, repotted, and pinched off dead leaves with lightning speed.

Her long slender fingers frequently greeted each other in clasping hugs and twisting worry about money and bills. In response to a limited income in our family, my mother's hands wove, clipped, and glued bric-a-brac to round metal backings that she fashioned into earrings to sell at the church bazaar.

I first realized my mother was aging by looking at her hands. She had the gift of soft skin and an unlined face well into her seventies. My parents' retirement home in North Carolina was surrounded with plants inside and out. The house, of course, was spotless due to the Saturday morning vacuuming and dusting done by a house-cleaner *after* Mother had cleaned and straightened in readiness for her arrival.

Sitting across from my mother at her kitchen table in Carolina, I watched in fascination as she smoothed Pond's hand cream around and around her palms, up and down each finger, over each short, clipped nail. Years of Pond's cream and good genes kept the skin smooth, but years also brought randomly placed brown age spots, purple-blue veins, and bumps at knuckles where arthritis lived.

"Do your hands hurt here?" I asked, reaching with one of my younger hands to touch a crooked index finger. We looked at that finger. I saw my mother's hand in mine. She was seventy-three; I was forty-three.

"No. No." Her hand withdrew from mine as she stood up with a burst of energy. Her hands moved our teacups to the sink.

Seven years passed. My father had died and my mother was visiting me. We were going out to lunch. Her hand reached out to hold mine for balance as we moved up the steps to the restaurant. Veins made a map on the back of her hand; the age spots had merged into dark tannish shapes. Her smooth skin felt like tissue paper in mine, and there was a tremor flicking under the thin surface.

My mother was old. I looked at my own hand. The skin was smooth, with small funny "freckles," as my grandson called them, dotting the backs. My nails were cut short and unpolished. *I had my mother's hands.*

When I turned fifty, my husband started teasing me about getting old.

"No. I'll never get old. Look at my mom. She looks really young and she's eighty."

Then when my mother was eighty-four, a rogue blood clot that had nestled near her brain decided to migrate, and then burst. A hemorrhagic stroke, the doctor said.

Her hands no longer partnered each other in Pond's application. We moved her to New Jersey where nurses, aides, and my sisters and I washed, combed, and gave eye drops and feedings. In visiting my mother almost every day for the five years of her post-stroke life, I saw the right side of her body give up the fight. Her right hand curled with atrophy.

But her left hand was the barometer for her moods—anxiously picking at her clothing or waving gracefully in the air to the sounds of her Glenn Miller CD.

One day I was so fatigued from doctor calls, Medicare research, worry, visits, and trying to have a life that I merely sat next to her bed and put my head down in her lap.

And the miracle happened. My mother's left hand lightly touched my hair, then slid down to my neck, back to the top, and down again.

"You're a good daughter," I heard her say. My heart opened to any and all possibilities of how I could make my mother's remaining lifetime—a life.

Our efforts to go out doubled—me pushing her wheelchair, taking her shopping, to the park, watching her favorite DVDs—the old Bill Cosby stand-up routines, *Michael,* and anything with Fred Astaire and Ginger Rogers. We'd go down the hall greeting everyone in the nursing home.

"Say hi, Mom."

"They don't even hear us," she'd grumble.

"But we hear us, Mom, and that's the difference. Put out your left hand. Say hello." This routine was repeated by all three of my mother's daughters on our visits to her nursing home. We called it *the mano-a-mano,* and soon the residents were reaching out as we approached.

Mom reached out her hand whenever she had a visitor, be it her family, the nurse, her doctor, or as time went by, the hospice aide. Mano-a-mano extended to handholding accompanied by a slight patting from her old, tired hand.

Handholding in the activity room became hand kissing. Here was a population bound to their wheelchairs, but the hands of her fellow residents reached out to each other and then lifted to lips or cheeks.

Her last winter, Mom would take my hand as soon as I got to her room and hold tight.

"Let's go see how everyone is." Her cue to do the mano-a-mano thing. Gradually her speech faded to one-word answers. But her hand held always tight.

One night during the holidays, I was called to the nursing home. "Your mother is having complications."

Her room was almost dark. One small yellow light cast soft shadows on the Christmas decorations my sister and I had put up, with Mom indicating where with a final directorial wave of her hand.

She took my hand as I sat by her bed. I gave it a squeeze. No squeeze back. She looked at me, uncurled her hand from my grasp and slid it around to the top of mine. Still holding my gaze, I felt one pat, and then she gently pushed my hand away.

My mother died three nights later on Christmas Eve—exactly five years to the day that she had had her stroke.

I like to believe she is in the care of hands that will always be gentle and loving, and her hands will return the love.

PEGASUS

Watching my mother's reactions to looking at old photos gave me a clue to possible stories. When she paused while looking at the Pegasus photo, I reached for my pen and paper.

In the last year of my mother's life, our hospice angels recommended bringing in photo albums to assist my mother in her "life review." Some pictures brought a smile, some a short sniff of dismissal. Some elicited a story.

The black-and-white photo was faded—five young women grouped around an old 1934 Ford. Yet the sight of that photo, labeled Pegasus, brought a light into my mother's eyes that I hadn't seen in months.

Here is my story of her story.

In 1939 the five young women in the photo taught at Drew Seminary in Carmel, New York, where the Readers Digest Corporate offices are today. Some of the teachers are more formally listed in the 1939–40 Drew Seminary faculty and staff program as:

Carmel Benson—Math and Chemistry
Gladys Berberich—Latin
Martha Crowley—English
Norma Harvester—History
Agnes Hyatt—Piano Harmony and Organ

The five in the photo were part of a close group of girlfriends calling themselves "The Jolly Five." The camaraderie of the group was deepened by affectionate nicknames—"Aggie," "Harvey," "Moo," "Itchie," and "Benny." It was unusual for a young woman to have a college education in those days, and to be teaching. It was probably unusual for five women to undertake the investment they did in those days too.

Over the years, my mother, Gladys (Itchie), and Carmel (Benny) stayed in touch. The two friends wrote of their careers, children, then retirement, grandchildren, deaths of spouses, and births of great-grandchildren. Gradually their letters included memories and photos of their time together at Drew.

In 2002 I was invited into this intimate correspondence when I began to act as secretary for my eighty-four-year-old mother after she suffered the debilitating stroke that robbed her of writing and some speech abilities. I had heard of Benny over the years as a teacher friend at Drew Seminary where my mother had taught Latin. So I knew part of our correspondence would be to Benny in Massachusetts.

Birthday, Halloween, and Christmas cards came and went for several years. Then one day "Pegasus" arrived. My tiny aging mother reached out a thin and shaky hand to hold the faded photograph. She placed it down on the table where we were sitting. Then she smoothed her worn hand over the photo, back and forth, as if to absorb the memory into her skin.

Back in 1939, Benny had an invitation to teach math and science at Drew Seminary. In September she joined the faculty and soon was part of a happy crew of teachers and students. The little "gang" included five single female teachers.

Benny's Uncle Ed lived in Brewster, New York, the town next to Carmel. Uncle Ed knew of a good second-hand car available for fifty dollars. So the friends gathered funds and bought it—probably in 1940. They named the car "Pegasus." Like the Pegasus of Greek mythology, this Pegasus had wings to take the young teachers on weekend adventures.

Benny wrote, "Uncle Ed worked out the paperwork (insurance, etc.) and we had fun driving about shopping in nearby Danbury, Connecticut. A few times some of us drove to my hometown, Dover Plains, just thirty miles away. We parked it on campus in a place that wouldn't be in the way at Drew. We loved our Pegasus."

More unusual for me than my shy and quiet mother having a career was the realization that she had had her driver's license, as did Benny and Moo. She and her friends were independent beyond my imaginings.

These women continued to be ahead of their time, even financially. They eventually sold Pegasus for seventy-five dollars—making a financial profit to split amongst them.

Post Pegasus: I told this story to some women I know when we were talking about mothers. Everyone had her own mother story. Perhaps you'll have one to share.

A MOTHER'S GIFT

It was a relief to discover the variety and similarity of relationships my female friends have had with their mothers. Candy's story was the beginning thread for this story.

A few years ago I started walking at the mall with a friend. We met around 7:00 AM and walked several loops. A mile for each loop, the official mall walkers said. The faster we walked, the more we talked. A majority of the talks were about relationships, particularly mother-daughter.

We both had had our share of conflict with our mothers. I had been a rebellious teenager in the 1960s. I missed curfew, got caught smoking. Breaking rules seemed the only way I could move towards separation from my parents.

Fulfilling her mother's high expectations had made childhood difficult for my friend, Candy, too.

Our relationships had mellowed as our mothers got older and we gained insight into the perspective of our 1950s' moms; perfect children equaled perfect mothers, and imperfect children .... Well, you can see how it went.

Both Candy and I found our past conflicts with our moms had faded, replaced by a growing maturity and the common experience of caring for our aging mothers. We both witnessed these independent and often difficult women move into various stages of illness and vulnerability that comes with aging, sometimes with cranky or bitter resistance, sometimes with a sense of grace that was astounding and inspiring.

And as Candy and I had aged, there was also the realization: we were so much like our mothers. Then our mothers died. We were both motherless daughters.

"I have my mother's hands," Candy said, spreading her fingers out in front of her as we walked. "Arthritis," she said as she touched the bumps near her joints.

"Me too." I located the age spots and bumpy veins that speckled the backs of my hands. "And all those years I vowed I'd never be like my mom."

"Funny."

One morning, post walk, Candy beckoned me to her car. "I want to show you something."

Out of the trunk of her car she produced a needlepoint pillow, a kaleidoscope of colors sliding across in a vibrant collage.

"Wow," I breathed. I knew Candy did needlepoint, but I'd only seen delicate patterns on immaculate white backgrounds.

"Yeah, different for me," she chuckled. "I got the colors from my mother."

"Your mother?" I asked. *Wait, oh, this was embarrassing.* I was pretty sure her mom had died. I had sent a card, a book.

"Oh yes, she died," Candy said. "She died six months ago. I think of her every morning. I miss her."

Candy looked off with a smile as if she saw her mom in the distance, maybe walking toward us. I know she was telling this story to me, but it was as if she were back in the story too.

"When Mom died, my sister and I went to clean out her house. My sister found this box of needlepoint with all Mom's unfinished work and said there was more of a chance that I would make use of it than anyone else in the family." Candy looked at me and chuckled. "After years of resisting my mother extolling the benefits of needlepoint work to calm nervous thoughts and hands, I reluctantly tried it. It worked."

She glanced down at the reminder of her mother. "My mother did needlepoint for years," she said as her middle-aged hands smoothed across the pillow. "Everyone in the family has something by her. She had to stop when her arthritis became so painful. Maybe she thought she would start again, that's why she saved all this."

Candy's eyes met mine as the same thought occurred to us both. Maybe something made her save it for someone else.

It reminded me of the time I found my mother's journal from 2001 when my sisters and I were closing up her apartment in preparation to move her nearer to us. Entries from January to September included her dreams about my dad, reflections of her visits with her daughters, and her self-talk to get out and see people more. But in October and November of that year, the handwriting was shaky, dwindling to just two-sentence entries, some doctor visits, and then nothing at all in December. And that was the month she had her stroke.

Were the pillows and journal forgotten items? I think not. I felt a new closeness with my friend—her life paralleled mine.

Candy continued, "When I took the box home and went through the mix of threads and pillow forms, I found this one. It struck me because it was so colorful and had already been started. That's why I say my mom gave me the colors. I continued the pattern, and it's finished, but..." she said with a final pat, "we did it together."

"You know what I mean?" Candy asked aloud, but I sensed another question behind her words. "Do you understand how I feel?" I did.

What a lovely gift from your mother, I thought. The usually bubbly features of my friend's face softened as she bent over to pull out a second unfinished memory. I could see in her face the little girl, young woman, and now middle-aged woman who loved her mother as deeply as I had grown to love mine.

"Look at this. Green and red, almost finished. I like to imagine she was doing this one for me; there's so much red in my house. I'll do this one next—just in time for Christmas."

THE DOG DAYS OF SUMMER

My husband was positively haggard when he arrived home from work on the last Friday of August. For some, late August in the suburbs of the New York-New Jersey metropolitan area conjures a Disneyesque forest scene with those ubiquitous little white flowers and the incessant chirping of bluebirds carried on a soft summer breeze. A smiley sunshine looks down on green grass and lush trees, with perhaps a sprinkling of autumn orange or yellow.

Now if you live in New Jersey you know this is pure fantasy. The dog days of summer swarm like mosquitoes through the tri-state area. Roads are clogged with overheated cars and drivers. The sidewalks of New York City are stuffed with gawking tourists and resentful residents who just know the *real* New Yorkers are somewhere in the Hamptons self-indulgently slathering sunblock over every part of their bodies.

If you are a commuter on the New Jersey Transit, as my husband was, it means hot sticky trains and buses filled with suburbanites operating under the delusion that this Friday they will "get out of the city a little early." Don't even consider going underground and getting on a subway. The added element of cell phones held by commuters who require no boundaries for private conversation are makings for a commuter's nightmare.

As a cruel bonus of my husband's train ride, there was the TGIF group that played pinochle on the train complete with a song they made up about the jack of diamonds and the queen of spades. This was a rich concoction for the makings of a haggard honey arriving home. No Disney atmosphere here.

It's the dog days of summer. The name comes from the ancient Roman belief that Sirius, also called the Dog Star, which is in close proximity to the sun, was responsible for the hot weather and short tempers. The Romans considered Sirius to be the "Dog Star" because it is the brightest star in the constellation Canis Major, large dog. But I digress.

Hank limped into the house and leaned against the door, partly to shut it and partly to hold himself up.

"The dog days of summer are upon us," he pronounced.

Dog days were also popularly believed to be an evil time "when the seas boiled, wine turned sour, Quinto raged in anger, dogs grew mad, and all creatures became languid, causing to man burning fevers, hysterics, and phrensies" according to Brady's *Clavis Calendarium,* 1813. There may be some truth in this. Hank's story bears it out.

Let's go back to earlier in the day when Hank was still crisp and cool. His 8:30 AM staff meeting had gone well. There was some minor grumbling about the inconsistency of the air conditioning, but for the most part, things were "coming along"—code for "no disasters yet."

But in another department on the twenty-sixth floor of that same company, Rowena was uncomfortably hot. The vents were actually vibrating as the earlier cozy comfortable air now blasted a veritable heat wave down on her carefully coiffed beehive. The heat of the supposed AC threatened to melt the thin shellac that held her hairdo in place.

"It's hot," she murmured. She looked at the purple digital clock on her desk. 10:30. She'd been at her desk since 9:30 trying to work in this rising temperature, and now the sun was shining directly on her desk. She knew this was not an age-related, aka menopausal, symptom. Those days were long behind her. It was definitely the AC, or rather, lack of AC.

No one in the department could adjust the thermostats since some muckety-muck from Office Services had brackets placed over every thermostat on the twenty-sixth floor. Someone, whose name shall not be mentioned here, and who did not have the sense to use the brain the good Lord had given him, had jammed a pencil in the thermostat of Rowena's department in an effort to keep the temperature at sixty-eight degrees, for goodness' sake. As a result, each thermostat now had a little metal basket covering it like some atmospheric chastity belt.

Rowena looked at the clock again. 10:40. "Well, it's obvious I will have to do something," she muttered to no one in particular. "It appears nobody at Office Services is going to adjust the central AC." It was of little importance to Rowena that no one at Office Services had been told about the growing AC discomfort in her department.

"Alma, see if you can open the window some, will you, hon?"

Alma was Rowena's sidekick, lackey, and all around loyal friend for the twenty-three years they had worked together.

"But, Ro, we are not allowed to open the windows." Alma operated under the illusion that because she obeyed all rules, both sane and quirky, that her friend Rowena would too.

"Alma, I'm sweatin' bullets here. My hands are slidin' off the keyboard."

Alma tried again. "I do not know if I should do this." Alma became very formal in her speech when she knew she was getting into dangerous territory with Rowena. "I just got off of disability leave. My back, you know." And she moved her small bejeweled hand gingerly to her back.

"Oh, don't be such a wimp. Open the window."

To the human resources employee who tried to recreate this fiasco later on, the following scenario might have resembled something out of *The Three Stooges*. Three, because where Rowena was, Alma went. And where Alma and Rowena went, so also went the Someone of the pencil episode. Alma was required to aid and abet Rowena in her missions, and Someone went along to watch for the entertainment value.

Our HR observer would have seen a past-middle-age woman hunched by a window handle feverishly cranking as another woman and man alternately looked at the crank and then up near the ceiling. "It won't open. Oh, wait. There, I got it." Alma was breaking a slight sweat across her forehead.

"There you go. Just a smidge more, Alma."

There was a popping sound as the window handle broke off in pieces in Alma's hands.

Rowena, Alma, and Someone lined up to survey the window, actually a wall of windows, starting at a ledge about waist high and going up to the ceiling where a row of smaller windows graced the upper reaches of glass. Those who design windows for high buildings know about strong and determined characters like Rowena, and so the lower larger windows were cemented and epoxied in place and did not open. But the smaller ones up top could be cranked open for fresh air if necessary. There was a limit of safety in the openings, which Alma, in her exertions, had surpassed.

Never one to turn her back on a challenge, Rowena climbed up on her desk and stepped across a narrow gap to straddle window ledge and desk. HR Observer might have noted that the woman who was stretching, and it was an admirable stretch, to open the window because it was so hot in her office, still had on a heavy wool sweater.

"You there, make yourself useful. Hand me some paper. No! No, not that. Give me some from the recycle box. We want to be environmentally conscious." Rowena was feeling a bit frisky up there on the ledge.

A stack of recycling paper was relayed up to Rowena who wadded it up and crammed it in the opening to push the window open a bit more and keep it open. Alma was still holding the broken handle and commenced to cheer Rowena on. Rowena then felt prematurely victorious and turned to make a V sign, arms up and out. She had forgotten about that small gap between the desk and ledge.

"Uh oh," escaped from a watcher as soon as he saw Ro's V. "We're on the twenty-sixth floor."

Rowena's grin morphed into a grimace and she tilted over. And tottered toward the floor.

Alma jumped into action. She extended both arms to her friend. HR Observer would see Victory Woman fall into the waiting arms of the coworker recently returned from disability for a back injury.

Rowena and Alma hobbled off in each other's arms with their third party pulling up the rear to go make tea with honey for them in the air-conditioned cafeteria.

By 3:30 PM, aka two hours after lunch, Rowena's pain was unbearable. Her back-disabled colleague speed-dialed HR to send an accident report and a car to take her friend home.

At 4:10 PM, Hank, as VP-in-charge, got the report. His eyes scanned the paper. Employee fell at 10:45 AM. *Wait, 10:45 and now it's 4:10?* Rowena's later explanation about this time gap, "Bear with me here," begged the frazzled HR employee, was:

1. No way was she going to an ER. Last year, or was it the year before, her cousin waited fifteen hours in ER. He could have bled out on the floor with not so much as a glance from those people.

2. Her doctor, who had his office in her apartment building, only started his office hours at 2:00 PM.

Hank read further. Employee fell from open window. *In? Out?* He raced to Rowena's office expecting to see the hapless employee on the floor or a tragically empty and silent office.

There was quite a group gathered, kind of like how birds cluster around a birdbath even though there is no water in it, only this cluster was in front of the window.

"I didn't think Rowena was that tall," said Doreen from the cafeteria.

"Oh, yeah, she was on her high school basketball team," offered Cyndi from reception.

"Where's Rowena?" Hank asked as he got to the doorway. *What the hell is Cyndi from reception doing all the way over here?*

Selma from quality control turned, coffee cup in hand. "Oh, they called a car to take her home."

Hank took in the scene of the accident. Rowena's desk, ordinarily organized in neat piles of folders and papers, looked like a candidate for a clutter intervention. There was even recycled paper in the clean paper basket. The casement window handle was lying in two abandoned pieces on the floor. Wadded paper was stuffed in the window frame. The window, without the handle as its rudder, was now stuck in a very wide-open position.

"They're sayin' we're in for some mean T-storms tonight," Someone said. There were murmurs of "Oooh, messy" and "Ro's not gonna like this."

VP Hank realized unraveling this would take some time. The dog days of summer had arrived.

Genesis Revealed: I was party to an incident similar to the thermostat sabotage, and have also seen and heard about long-lasting work relationships where loyalty often surpasses logic. New York City in August brings about some fuzzy thinking. Add a character who usually tries to keep sanity intact in spite of overwhelming odds. A perfect recipe for "Dog Days of Summer."

YOU, ME, AND SOMEBODY

 It just happened too many times not to write about it.

When my husband and I moved to Tucson, it was a planned cross-country retirement trip. We had dreamed of this for years, first vacationing in Tucson, and then being courted by a local real estate agent.

During the retirement drive from New Jersey to Arizona, we reviewed our list of negotiable and nonnegotiable requirements in our soon-to-be-found dream home. Family room with open plan access to kitchen, high-ceiling living room with fireplace, dining room optional, two-car garage, spacious feel, and lots of windows for the Tucson light and sun. Three bedrooms—ours, a guest bedroom, and one as an office for my writing. We were empty nesters, with no children and no pets. Just the two of us.

Over our twenty years of marriage, we had crafted a way of living that allowed each of us to get pretty much whatever we wanted. Our life was very smooth. Cooking was minimal for both of us. However, we do like to eat, so often dined out. When we cooked, it was simple and pretty nutritious—a salad, veggies, and some protein in the form of chicken or fish. Steak, if Hank cooked. Neither of us was a pack rat or collector, so there was minimal clutter. We had developed ways to get along and maintain a beautiful home.

78

We did find our dream home and during the first year painted, furnished, decorated, and settled in. Just sweetie and me.

I don't know how it happened, but after about a year, we found we had a new resident. Neither of us had invited company. There was no "Welcome to our home." But it happened anyway.

One morning Hank said, "*Somebody* left the front door unlocked last night." Whoa, that sent a shiver of alarm through me. I looked from room to room. Nothing misplaced or missing. Hmm, oh well.

A few days later, my husband remarked, "Somebody left the cabinet doors open in the kitchen." Now I had just been in the kitchen that morning, doing a whirlwind stocking of shelves after a major Costco run. You know how the original Costco list of "just a few things" can blossom into a full-scale haul. All the food and the eighteen-roll packs of paper towels and toilet paper had been stored. And I had done all the unpacking myself. So who else was in the kitchen?

Then it struck me. Somebody was an elusive, passive, nonexistent entity. It was Hank's way of letting me know my chore was not finished to his satisfaction. Somebody roams freely in our home. Both my husband and I have seen evidence that Somebody has been in the house. I just know Somebody is often responsible for leaving lights on in unoccupied rooms. I have noticed, more than once, that Somebody often leaves the gunk in the kitchen drain, and has even eaten my very last bit of chocolate bar that was tucked way in the back of the refrigerator.

Somebody often wears the disguise of Who. Who is going to lock up tonight. Who divides his/her time between my house and my sister's. At my sister's house, Who is neglectful in the care and use of utilities. Who often leaves the water running, just a trickle, and the oven stays lit long after the roast is served.

It's only the two of us living in our house. This use of a generic unknown subject drives me crazy. Yet the words fall from my mouth like water over a dam. "Somebody left that hall light on again." And Hank counters with his own reply delivered in dulcet tones. "Well, I'm sure I don't know who. I guess Somebody will just have to remember to turn it off."

YOU GET WHAT YOU PAY FOR

After years of wrapping presents and cutting Christmas tags and realizing my sisters and I have the same recycling habits as my mother, I started writing about Christmas wrappings. When Hank experienced this brown shirt episode, it just added another bud to this story.

Hank and I were at a local wholesale clothing store one afternoon on an impromptu stop-off for last-minute vacation supplies. As we passed the sale rack for shirts, I lingered. "Why don't we get one of these for you?" I asked. "It's lightweight. Good for hot weather."

"No, keep moving," was Hank's response.

"But..."

Hank actually looked at the label, something he rarely does. "I will never forget this label," he said. "Remember that summer shirt your mother gave me years ago?"

The sting of past fiascos fades slowly. Years later we both could smile, but we both also remembered.

My usually calm husband had come home from work one humid summer evening and thrust both hands in front of me, palms up, and said, "Look at my hands." The palms of his hands were a streaked honey color. He then took off his jacket, ripped open his shirt, and beseeched, "Look at me."

81

Thinking this might be a new approach to intimacy, I gazed at him. His torso, though unclothed, looked as if he were wearing a long-sleeved, chestnut-colored shirt.

Then he spoke, "It's the dye from that shirt your mother gave me last Christmas." And so it was. Hank was a living example of my father's money concept, "You get what you pay for." More to the point, Hank was a victim of my mother's frugality program.

My mother always loved a bargain. Her definition of a bargain seemed to be the lower the cost, the better the deal—even if it meant sacrificing quality, in this case, that colorfast characteristic.

My mother's money-managing strategy had been honed over the years. Its foundation was built on the Depression of the 1930s. Money *was* really scarce. Marrying my dad furthered the idea of frugality as neither of them had any money to spare in 1941.

However, they were resourceful and resilient.

The magic of Christmas during my childhood in the 1950s was in the transformation of the pitifully thin tree my dad would bring home and the resulting thickly branched Christmas tree he set up in the living room. Accompanied by a lot of verbal exhortations of "Ding dang it, get in there, you," Dad could make a scrawny Christmas tree positively grow like the tree in the *Nutcracker* ballet with the use of a drill and a few strategically placed scrap branches.

Mom learned to put together all kinds of highly nutritious, low-cost, sometimes low-on-taste meals. One regular on her menu, my nightmare, was hot dogs and lima beans in tomato sauce. "But it's the Christmas colors" might have been her justification.

From childhood, my sisters and I heard the family money mantras of "Turn off the lights," "Don't use all the hot water," along with botany lessons about what did and did not grow on trees and the biology lesson about what Dad was not made of. We ate everything on our plates, not only for the starving children in Europe, but because, "I paid *good* money for that food." There was no such thing as *bad* money in our house. In fact, there seemed to be very little money at all.

Occasionally my father would lose it and buy something extravagant. What a gleeful time for us when he came home with our first television set, a small-screen black-and-white TV! I remember watching *Sheena, Queen of the Jungle*, my high-nutrition-low-taste dinner on a TV table in front of me, while my mother lay in the bedroom recovering from this purchase as well as my father's unthinkable statement, "It's only money."

I got used to the food. I learned how to clip coupons. Each summer my sisters and I set up a cottage industry in the basement, sewing our clothes for the coming school year. But I could never, ever get used to a shallow bath in tepid, no—not even tepid, water. To this day I take long hot, hot showers with little regard to how pruned my fingers get.

Over the years, my parents' financial situation improved. They were able to afford a first car and then a second. When my twin sister and I were seniors in college, Mother and Dad took a trip to Europe. They had arrived!

But old habits die hard.

During a summer visit to my parents' cozy retirement home in North Carolina, my husband and I basked in the sun on the deck. We relaxed inside in air-conditioned comfort. But when it came time to take a shower, we learned economy water savers do work and can be operated overtime in North Carolina.

Mother feigned not understanding why there was no hot water for a shower. I mentioned this to my twin sister on the phone.

"Ah, you need to find the water saver switch. Go downstairs, under the stairwell, behind the furnace. It can be on a timer but she probably has it off all day. Find the blue switch. Hit it. Blue light— hot water's on; no light—hot water's off."

A casual conversation with my mother revealed that, yes, she and Dad had purchased the water saver, which was linked to the hot water heater. Negotiations ensued. We agreed to use the timer. From 11 PM to 10 AM the hot water would be off. From 10 AM to 1 PM the hot water would be on. Pleasant option: If my husband and I wanted more hot water, we could shower together.

Next day as I was on my way to the shower, I saw my mother

scampering up the basement stairs. She sashayed into the kitchen. I scampered down the stairs. No light. Hot water was off. I scampered up.

"Mom, did you turn the hot water heater off?"

She looked me right in the eye and said, "No."

I regressed to parent-child behavior. I whined, "Mom."

She dug in her heels. "We," (notice the royal "we") "just don't need all that hot water. That bill will be too high. Your father's not made out of money, you know."

Several years before the brown shirt fiasco, my husband took my dad out to do his Christmas shopping for my mother. Dad knew exactly what he wanted to buy—a pink flannel nightgown. Upper-end stores and boutique shopping were promptly rejected. Only at a discount department store did a smile light up Dad's face, but it vanished when he looked at the price tag.

"Eleven dollars. Mother would kill me if she knew I spent this much on her."

Hank scrambled through the sale bin to beat that price. They did. As he told this to me later getting ready for bed, he paused, one shoe in hand, looking blankly at the floor. "I thought we would never leave the mall. I thought we would have just been there forever."

In our adult years, when the Christmas glut arrived, there were piles of packages, much ripping of wrapping paper and flinging of bows and ribbons. But even this seeming frivolity was seasoned with the flavor of my mother's economic program. A woman ahead of the times, she would have made environmentalists burst with pride. She couldn't resist exhorting us to refashion and reuse every ribbon, bow, and tag. A noble idea, but even reused paper has a certain shelf life. Her own gift tags were recycled Christmas cards. Definitely a clever idea, the kind featured in craft magazines today. Pictures of wreaths,

Santas, elves, and reindeer were snipped and cut with pinking shears so the edges were zigzagged, with our names written on the front. The bonus was the remaining part of the note written by the card sender on the back from previous holidays. So the back of a card read something like this:

-Earline and I went out to Arizo-
-see the kids. 4 grandkids now. Earl's hearing is givi-
-ouble but we still get our weekly game of-

As Hank opened his present from Mom that last Christmas, the now famous brown shirt tumbled away from mounds of tissue paper. Mother's hands reached out to smooth the paper for next year's use.

"There's mileage in that paper."

Hank held on to the paper jealously. "This is not only my gift, it's my paper and bow. I know, because I wrapped your present with it last year."

He may see it again because I have it in the recycling box in our attic along with a great book I got for him at The Book Exchange. Only four dollars. What a deal!

After my father passed away, my mother continued living alone in Carolina. Ever the economist, she reasoned, "If something happens to me and I can't take care of myself, I'll move up by my girls. But for now I want to stay here in Carolina. This has been our home for twenty years. Besides it's cheaper to live here than up North." And so she did. She managed her home and money smoothly, seemingly with no break in the frugality of her married years.

About a year after my dad passed away, I had an interesting conversation with her over the phone. "It's sometimes lonely here. I'm ready to get out more. I thought I'd take a small vacation," she said.

"That's great, Mom. It will be good for you to get out and meet

people. What are you planning? A bus trip to Ashville? Amtrak up to Williamsburg?"

"Sort of. I booked a luxury Caribbean cruise."

"A cruise!" I squeaked. "Isn't that going to be rather expensive?"

"Oh, I don't know," she replied. "It's only money."

A Rose for Karen

Alcoholism is an equal opportunity disease. My friend gave me the seed for this story over ten years ago, telling me about his daughter and his recovered relationship with her in the last years of her life. Other friends gave me the shoots that added drinking loneliness and the day-after coldness, the torn loyalties of children, and the exquisite gift of forgiveness. When a dear friend died from alcoholism, I had to write this from the father's point of view to share the possibilities of family healing in recovery.

March—St. Patrick's Day:

I tapped on the door and entered the quiet room. Karen looked up from her journal. Smiling, she slipped the notebook into the bedside dresser drawer. My heart gave a small thump at the smile she gave me.

I still can't get over this. My daughter smiling, lifting her head for my kiss on her forehead. *How many kisses had gone ungiven? How many times was she waiting for that kiss and I wasn't there?*

"How are you today?" I fluffed the pillows and sat by her bed.

"Today is okay," came Karen's answer.

Okay. Flat voice under the smile. Okay was an increasingly relative term. Last month okay meant "I got out of bed today." This month okay was the code word for "the chemo hasn't knocked me out."

"We're gonna beat this, Pumpkin," I said as I pulled up a chair by the bed.

So began my weekend as a father of an adult daughter who had been stricken with cancer at the age of twenty. I picked up a book and began to read as my lovely daughter looked at me intently. We're going through the classics.

"I missed them in high school," she had told me. "Remember? No, I guess you don't. Mom used to go down to school when I got in trouble for cutting."

This said in a matter-of-fact tone. *Why is she not angry with me for the void of her childhood when I was involved in my love affair with alcohol?* Like the breeze flipping the pages of the book on the windowsill, I scrolled back in time. Not only did I miss protecting her from impulsive actions like cutting school, I missed the junior high dance recital, the high school music concert. By high school graduation, there was no pretense of why Dad was missing from the smiling picture of relatives flanked protectively around the blue-capped beauty that was my daughter.

"I used to cut classes a lot," continued Karen, unaware of my mental wandering, "and I only know bits of Shakespeare, Thomas Wolfe, and Daphne du Maurier. Now I want the whole thing."

And so I began to read. "Last night I dreamt I went to Manderley again..."

June—Father's Day:

You know, you can read aloud and have an inner dialogue going on at the same time. We've finished *Rebecca* and now are on *Robin Hood*.

How did this awful disease happen to my daughter? But we'll beat this. My mantra.

I am no longer the absent father chasing grandiose dreams, drowning hurts in yet another cheap bottle of scotch. For years, the imagined slights of my colleagues had the power to send me out to the bar after work. The twinkling lights of Buddy's Place were soft and friendly. The air-conditioning was a cooling balm for my hot temper and hurt feelings. These were my friends. "Here, let me buy this round. You like me, right? I have friends here, right?" Not those grinds at the office. When the last of my "friends" had vanished home to their families, the lights at Buddy's were harsh; the air was stale with smoke and spilled beer.

Today, no more the repetition of the thin and brittle excuses delivered in Karen's childhood. "Daddy had to work late. He'll come to your next recital. I promise, Pumpkin."

Coming out of a blackout to see my little girl's pale face, eyes looking bigger and darker than ever as she peered down at me from the stairway. "Daddy's sick again, Mommy." The only answer to her report was the sound of the bedroom door closing as my wife retreated to the loneliness of her bed.

I knew with desperate predictability the scenario of the morning after. I would again get up early, stand under the showerhead for twenty minutes, soaking up water to give some life to my body. Then I would whistle as I cooked a huge breakfast of bacon, eggs, toast, and fresh-squeezed juice. Not for me, but a curtain of food to cover the coldness, the emptiness, the void as Karen came quietly out of her room, a reluctant actor on the stage of the day after.

"Breakfast is ready. Sit here. It's a great day," I'd say with a heartiness I did not feel. "Karen, when you finish I'll take you down to the park." This to avoid meeting my wife's gaze. We moved in the kitchen without touching, without speaking to each other. Her coldness was a different cooling from the air-conditioning of the night before. This was a coldness born of frustration, defeat, and now a growing hatred. "You have to leave before Karen hates you as much as I do," was all she said that day.

And there was Karen, stuck in the middle. "Dad, Joe called. He said to come get your car. Do you even know where it is?"

Now my ex-wife does the caregiving for Karen each evening during the week. On Friday evenings, I arrive at Karen's tiny sunny apartment with my old black gym bag packed with a toothbrush, workout clothes, and the latest gleanings from the youth section of the local library. I see my daughter; I actually see her with clear eyes, a clear head, and a sober body and spirit.

But still I am angry. Now, not at myself, but at this other disease over which the experts say we have no control. We've scoured the coast for the best doctors. Our friends' prayers and spiritual messages swirl around us in the center of this small universe that is Karen. Our sun. Strength in numbers! We'll beat this! You'll see!

September—Labor Day weekend:

Helen, our hospice angel, says I must get some rest. "Go out to dinner. Rent a video. Go for a walk. Get out of this apartment."

She looks at me blankly when I respond, "But I've already done that. For years and years I was out of the house, out for a walk, out of her life. How can I do that now when she may so soon be out of mine?"

November—Thanksgiving:

I am numb. I am filled with fear disguised as anger. I bargain with God. *If You take this from Karen, I will never lose my temper again. I will never argue with my ex again.*

I have no sense of thanksgiving.

December:

Our Karen is gone. I am staring blankly at her address book. My hand, which holds the phone, seems limp and detached from the me that is the father of this darling girl. Her mother's gone to "make the arrangements." I get to make the phone calls. How can I do this? What do I say? Our prayers weren't enough to keep her here. She's gone. Cancer won.

I feel such frustration. Anger. Rage. I fling the pathetic little address book at the wall. The mosaic of Karen's life is shattered. My masterpiece mosaic for our adult relationship lies unfinished. I didn't have enough time to repair the childhood damage, to make up for the unsaid good-nights, the unread classics. These incomplete activities are like shiny, brittle pieces of the mosaic swept to the floor by a careless hand. Months of reading by her sickbed couldn't erase the unread bedtime stories of childhood, could they?

Not fair, God. Why did she die? Why did I live?

December—Christmas:

I raged through the wake. Friends came to pay respects. I was sober but sarcastic. My ex-wife gleaned comfort from looking at childhood pictures of Karen. Photos from which I was glaringly absent.

December—New Year's:

During the funeral I raged, but inwardly. Family came to say good-bye. I greeted them with a closed and locked heart. With Karen's high school and college friends, I could barely say hello. As I left the cemetery, my heart opened enough to break a single darkened rose from one arrangement that lay scattered like a favorite picnic blanket hurriedly forgotten in a storm. Later that night I placed it between tissues to press and mount.

Fool! Pressing flowers. What will that do? Will that ease this piercing pain? Will that stop the tears that come unbidden in the most unlikely places? Will that bring her back to us?

I tossed the tissue-wrapped flower carelessly in the first book in my path.

February—Valentine's Day:

She's gone. Stop my heart from hurting.

March—St. Patrick's Day:

I overheard my nephew's favorite retort to his sister when she complained about his teasing, "Oh, get over it."

But I couldn't get over it. My anger seeped like the water that spills over the top of a slowly overflowing bowl, to every corner of my life. Work was unbearable. I felt a physical pain below my heart when

I heard laughter. I isolated myself from friends who were enjoying life. My recovery meetings were the puddles of sanity that kept my fury from flooding. I was grieving and resisting at the same time. Two steps forward and one step back.

May—Mother's Day:

Closing up Karen's apartment, my ex-wife and I began the physical review of going though Karen's personal things. "I'll do this," I muttered. "Don't go over there on Mother's Day."

"No," she said. "It will be okay." So we went to find new homes for the pieces of our daughter's life. "Give this rocker to Sue, she always loved sitting here. These dishes go to the shelter."

"What do you want to do with this?" my ex asked. She was pointing to a framed copy of "Footprints," the poem Karen introduced me to in my early recovery. "Your Higher Power will carry you even when you cannot see the footprints in the sand," Karen had said.

The movement was so automatic I barely remember lifting my hand. The frame was off the wall and tossed into the wastebasket without a word passing between us. My sobriety taught me to view anger as a luxury of more balanced men. But now I was nowhere near balanced.

Sorting memories. "Look, here's her Pooh Bear. She had him since she was seven."

The copy of *Robin Hood*, spine now creased from our weekend readings, cover fading in the window-seat sun. "Take that back to the library," said my ex. Instead, I slipped it into my gym bag.

"Here. Read this." My ex tossed a brown leather-bound book to me. "Read this," she repeated. "You're in it."

Ha, some criticizing tactic of hers.

I looked at the title. "My Gratitude Book" by Karen. *Ha, again.* What did Karen have to be grateful for? Probably one of those sappy self-help books. Wasn't it like Karen to use a bright pink pen. I opened the book. Recovery phrases slashed like pink neon across a page in her backward-slanting handwriting.

Who are you to say there is no God?

G.O.D.—Good Orderly Direction

G.O.D.—Gratitude Once Daily

Put Gratitude In Your Attitude.

Let Go Let God.

Turn It Over.

Then on the next page—"My Gratitude List" by Karen

My daughter kept a gratitude list? When? The dates in the leather-bound book chronicled the last months of her life—her painful, suffering, reduced-quality life.

And there, partway down the list was... *I'm grateful for the relationship with my father. Now I have a dad.*

June—Father's Day:

I'm grateful for the relationship with my father. Now I have a dad.

I'm thinking of that again today. In retrospect, my rage broke up that day in May. As I read that list over and over, a crack began to split down my impenetrable wall of anger and bitterness.

Dear God, her life reduced, yes. But her spirit, oh that wonderful smiling spirit still loving and accepting. And she accepted me when I reentered her life. Thank you, Karen.

September—Labor Day:

I've since pondered "get over it." Get over it, as if life were a mountain to scale, an arduous uphill battle. I move through life protected by my Higher Power. The poem "Footprints" comes to mind again. Perhaps, just perhaps, this is true for me. God is taking care of me even though I don't see it. Well, I don't wholly believe this, but I'm now willing to "act as if."

December—Winter:

One of those tedious days at work. The techs were out. The boss was in. Tension was up. The computers were down. That night I reached for a technical manual at home, *Computers for Dummies.* The book opened to a flat tissue package pressed in between the pages. Karen's rose, so small and compact, had been protected in that soft tissue.

Oh, my lovely daughter. I hope you are at peace.

I glanced down at the date winking at me on my computer screen as if the irony of the upcoming numerical joke were already known to the digital world. Exactly one year to the day that she died.

January—A New Beginning:

Oh, my lovely rose daughter. Thank you. I believe I can be at peace too. I closed Karen's brown leather-bound book and slid it into my bedside dresser drawer.

SUMMER STOCK

Following a book discussion about my first book, Thinking of Miller Place: A Memoir of Summer Comfort, *the talk turned to summers. Marcia Dobler Levine shared her summer job story in her own hilarious, mock-serious tone. I added memories of vacations in the Catskills and Adirondacks for details in the setting and characters, and the remembered rush of that first crush.*

The summer they were sixteen, Marcia and Gail got jobs together—after all, they were best friends. In 1958 teenage girls were inseparable, that is until one of them got a boyfriend. Then it was as if they went underground with said boyfriend, never to be seen again.

Marcia and Gail's place of employment was in Monticello, New York, in the heart of the Catskill Mountains when the Catskills were in their resort center heyday. Monday through Friday, Marcia and Gail were held captive at R&S, an auto supply and toy store.

Yes, an odd combination of merchandise. But as the co-founder, Sidney Kornbaum Sr. said, "None of this specialty store stuff for me. Uncle Roy and Aunt Vern, God rest their poor worn-out souls, ran that toy store all through the Great Depression and left it to me. Thanks to my father-in-law, I have a solid connection with the wholesale auto guys. And I'm good at sales. So, we make do with the inventory we got."

The summer Marcia and Gail worked at R&S, Sidney Kornbaum Jr. was the proprietor, as he liked to remind everyone numerous times during the day. He had finally moved up from being the boss's son to the proprietor when Big Sid, as Sidney Kornbaum Sr. was known, and the wife, Harriet, decided they had had enough of being snowbirds, back and forth, Miami to Monticello, and "flew the coop" to Miami—permanently.

Big Sid was big in more ways than one. Big voice, big ideas, six feet three inches of solid mass, big assertive personality tempered by a big generous smile. Within a year of retirement, Big Sid was president of the Bay View Park HOA, Miami's leading snowbird community. Harriet reigned as the Bay View doyenne of fashion. She still went to New York City seasonally to buy her wardrobe. She triumphantly wore her white dotted Swiss cover-ups ten months of the year, Memorial Day and Labor Day fashion decrees be damned.

Sidney Jr. was Harriet and Big Sid's only and genetically weakened offspring. Slight, thin, and having reached his adult height of five-foot-four at seventeen, Sidney Jr. had some pretty big shoes to fill when his father turned over the reins of R&S to him. Junior flitted back and forth between gruffly reminding everyone of the rules and trying too hard to be friendly.

"Greetings, Marcia and Gail." Then he'd launch into his favorite song, "Oo ee, oo ah ah, ting tang, walla walla bing bang." He'd slap his hand on the counter to get their attention because they never looked at him if they could help it. "Heh, heh. 'Witch Doctor.' You girls know that one?"

There was something strange about having a boss who looked as young as they were and wore polka dot bow ties thinking it made him more like Winston Churchill. Churchill *had* often worn a polka dot tie, but with confidence. All Marcia and Gail could see in Sidney Jr.'s fashion statement was a confused mix of Charlie Chaplin and Jerry Lewis.

"Oh no, here he comes."

The slap, the toothy grin, and Sidney Jr.'s feeble laugh as he waggled his eyebrows at them.

Sidney Jr. kept the same employee rules his father had initiated back in the 1940s when he decided to hire kids during the summer months.

Rule #1. Hours: The store opened at 9:00 AM and closed at 4:30 PM, but work hours were 8:30 AM to 5:00 PM.

Rule #2. Dress code: All employees wore the R&S uniform. Boys: Dark green khaki trousers, white sneakers, and a dark green short-sleeved shirt with R&S embroidered in gold on the breast pocket. Girls: Dark green shirtwaist dress with flared skirt, accessorized with a darling white collar and cuffs designed by Mrs. K. Sr. The R&S was embroidered on the white collar of the dress in small gold letters.

Mrs. K. was adamant about not having the letters on the breast pocket of the dress. "There will be no eyes drawn to the chest area." The girls' uniform was completed with stockings and polished white flats.

Their uniforms fit quite nicely over the girls' slender figures and matched both Marcia's and Gail's coloring, so okay, they would wear the uniform. The problem came with the dress material, and wearing stockings. The sad fact was that R&S, although neat and spacious, was often dusty and not air-conditioned. If you have ever been on the East Coast in summer, you know what I mean. When outside temperatures were in the nineties, it seemed like a hundred degrees inside R&S. The fitted dress felt like heavy cotton swaddling around their bodies. Sticky stockings encased feet and legs and sucked the life out of any thought of feeling grown-up or sexy, even if the color was labeled nude.

Humidity can wreak havoc with hairdos. If your hair was naturally curly, as in Marcia's case, you could almost feel the curls climbing up and tightening on your head. If your hair was naturally blond, and perfectly straight, as in Gail's case, the effort of hours of sleeping in pin curls to produce ringlets was undone in twenty-five minutes. Your ringlets unraveled from adorable curls to loose waves. Clumps of hair hung flat against your head, weighted down with the generous amount of now-useless Aqua Net hairspray.

Your skin felt moist to the touch until you stacked several boxes up onto the top shelf in the store. Then you had a combination of fine dust mixed with humidity on your arms, hands, and worst of all, your face and neck. One morning Gail experimented with eyebrow pencil. Remember, natural blond hair means light blond eyebrows. So out came the Maybelline ebony-black pencil to darken her eyebrows. In the heat, humidity, and no air-conditioning of R&S, she wiped her forehead with the back of her hand. The result was a brown-black smear from left to right, giving her a unibrow look.

"Gail," said Marcia with a vigorous nod to the lavatory. "Bathroom break. Makeup rescue."

Rule #3. Salary: For all of the above, and standing on your feet for all those hours, you got paid a dollar an hour.

Rule #4. Girls were pointedly told this additional rule: "You cannot talk to the boys." It would mean instant dismissal. More on that later.

Rule #5. Lunch was 12:00 to 12:45 PM. All employees ate in a separate area in the stockroom where there were two long wooden tables. Girls ate lunch with each other at the girls' table. Remember, this was 1958; you had to be at least fifty to be a woman. Boys and men ate at the other wooden table. Mrs. Kornbaum Jr. continued Mrs. K. Sr.'s tradition of linen tablecloths—pink you know where, and a masculine navy blue for the men and boys.

Rule #6. Work areas: Girls worked up front at the counters or cash register. They became quite knowledgeable about toy manufacturing companies and appropriate ages for games. "Chutes and Ladders" yes, for five-year-olds. "Sorry" was good for any age on a rainy afternoon when you wanted to get revenge on a bratty little brother but could only do so with a sarcastic "Sorry" as you slammed his player piece back on Start.

Marcia and Gail could demonstrate how to use a hula-hoop while reading the latest Nancy Drew book, although doing this in the front store window as a promotional idea was nixed immediately by Mrs. K. Jr. "Dancing? Like floozies? Never!"

Their store knowledge was completed with the ability to rattle off tire brands and sizes and do tax calculations in their heads.

Stock boys, truck drivers, and unloaders—all male—worked in the mechanics shop and tire and toy stockroom.

So as far as talking with the boys, it was pretty much a safe bet that there would not be any "fraternizing," as Sid Jr. put it. It must be noted that although "Witch Doctor" was Sidney Jr.'s theme song, Peggy Lee's "Fever" ruled all teenagers' hormones in the summer of 1958. Weigh following hormones up against rules and it's easy to see which way the teenage scale will tip.

All went smoothly until Mel Schwartz was hired to work as a stock boy. "A handsome boy," Mrs. Sid Jr. noted with hooded eyes going from Mel to her "pigeons," as she protectively called Marcia and Gail. Mel was hired because he was a football player and was bound to be strong enough to unload incoming inventory. His additional responsibility was to unpack the inventory, move any boxes that were put on the staging floor to the front room, and bring the product and order form to either Marcia or Gail for a signature.

Now these were bright high school kids. They knew that "no talking with the boys" meant there was *permissible* conversation and *unacceptable* conversation.

Permissible:

Mel: Hi, Marcia. Here are the doll boxes from the staging area.

Marcia: Thanks, Mel. Do you have the order form for me to sign?

Mel: Why yes, Marcia. Here it is.

Marcia (signing the form): Thank you, Mel.

One bright sunny morning when there happened to be low

humidity so Marcia and Gail's tresses were behaving, Mel appeared, almost hidden by the four huge boxes he carried as if bearing gifts to the front-room green dress goddesses.

It must be pointed out that Mel Schwartz also happened to be *the* high school heartthrob.

What put Gail's job in jeopardy was Mel using his bar mitzvah-trained voice to hum "Chantilly Lace" as he came through the swinging doors of the stockroom. He wisely or unwisely chose to shift from humming to singing the lyrics as he reached the counter. His dark curly hair, then mischievous eyes, then very handsome face, then neck, then football-conditioned torso appeared before Gail as he unstacked the boxes. And she heard, "Chantilly lace, and a pretty face and a pony tail hangin' down." He winked at her. "A wiggle in her walk and a giggle in her talk ..."

Of course, Gail giggled on cue.

Mel (bearing trouble as well as boxes): 'Morning, Chantilly. Here are four cartons just for you.

Gail (holding to the rules for a few brief seconds): Thanks, Mel. Do you have the order form?

Mel: For you, I've got anything you want.

Marcia moved closer to the counter. She could see Gail was in danger of breaking the no-talk rule. She could see it by the way their heads were bending close over the innocent, but incriminating, order form.

Mel (offering a worn #2 pencil): Sign right here.

And here, my friends, is where permissible crashed through the boundary line into unacceptable. Mel's index finger touched Gail's hand as he pointed to the signature box.

From her observation point, Marcia could see Gail blush, and she did not move her hand from Mel's reach. *Fever!* thought Marcia.

Mel: Your hair looks really pretty today, Gail.

Uh oh. Marcia moved in to intervene. She shook her head at Gail, making like "No, no, don't talk to him." Gail actually turned her body *away* from Marcia.

And then Marcia heard … "Oo ee, oo ah ah, ting tang, walla walla …"

Marcia and Gail both froze. The index finger of Mel Schwartz, high school heartthrob, still touched Gail's hand.

"Mel!" shouted Mr. Sidney Kornbaum Jr. "Back room."

Mel casually slid the #2 pencil behind his ear and sauntered away, whistling "Chantilly Lace."

Sidney Jr.'s voice shook with emotion, whether of true outrage or the thought of actually having to fire someone. "Gail. My office."

As it often goes, Mel got a mere banishment to the stockroom. And Gail lost her job.

"I thought the witch doctor was gonna cry," Gail told Marcia as she emptied her locker. "Self-righteous twerp. Or maybe he was really 'discomforted,' as he said, that he had to fire me. Nah." She slammed the locker door. "He said he was doing me a favor rounding off my final salary to the next dollar."

Her exit was a hugely defiant gesture. She left R&S by going out through the stockroom and men-only unloading area where Mel gallantly steered her on the R&S flatbed hand truck out to her bicycle.

Marcia was promoted to front office manager, a thinly disguised ruse to compensate for her working alone up front in the store, and she had to accept boxes and orders from old Karl Redman for the rest of the hot, dusty R&S summer.

And Gail, you ask? Gail got a job as a secretary in an air-conditioned office on Allen Street where she *sat* at a desk all day right up to Labor Day weekend.

P.S. At a later date, Marcia was inclined to share that she was going out with a boy named Mel.

LOW GEAR

Thanks to Colleen, who told me about her epiphany in a rented car. "She" of "Low Gear" is a composite of student teachers who arrived late to my classroom, my neighbor, and other sweet young things.

When she told me the transmission went on her car, I have to admit I was a tad disbelieving.

"I mean, it was like, totally unexpected," she told me, eyes wide with the shock of life's chicanery.

"Aren't there supposed to be clunks and dragging noises for those days before when you keep saying, 'I have to have that looked at'?" I asked in a casual voice. After all, this was the same young woman who never checked any car fluids at all. Certainly she must have had some auditory clues. I admit to a degree of irritation with her, which I found hard to disguise. Why was that? Why didn't she just have the car checked periodically? Of course! She reminded me of me, thirty years ago.

In my first years as a teacher, I had a thirty-mile commute from New York City to a lovely suburban town in New Jersey. My dad had given me reminders and training about my used Plymouth Sport Fury—check the oil, put air in the tires, and know what's under the hood. Yet, never once did I pop that latch to do any of it. What I did do was befriend Mr. D., a local mechanic who repaired cars as a side job in his garage. After coming to rescue me three times when I was stranded on the side of the road, Mr. D. began to call me seasonally. "Get your car over here for a check-up." He was my fairy godfather of auto land.

So why should my dear, lovely, flighty neighbor be any different? In addition, this seemed to be the worst financial period in her life. College loan payments lurked around every calendar page; the divorce from the it-will-never-last marriage was final, bringing emotional prosperity along with a one-salary standard of living. She never had enough money to take care of the car. But, you know, her nails were always manicured and polished.

After being stranded and wrapped in self-pity for days without any car, she called around for cheap rental rates. The lowest price that fit her budget was at a place that should have been called Rent-a-Car Facsimile.

"When do you open?"

"Six-thirty."

"I'll be there." Then she called me.

Recognizing this automotive denial phase from my own experiences, I agreed to help, and set the alarm for 6:00 AM, picked her up, and dropped her at the rental office. My compassion was but a thin veneer since I drove away before she even got in the door of the rental place, thus sealing her fate to accept whatever vehicle she was given.

The car they presented was smaller than her bathroom, which was pretty tiny. It had no radio and no power steering. It was bright red with a yellow interior. The sales associate, Hal, actually thought it helped to call the colors ketchup and mustard. Hal described the car as a coupé to evoke a sportier appeal. No dice, Hal. This was a really small car, with no AC either.

The previous renter must have smoked five cartons of cigarettes at one time. Later that evening when our mutual neighbor saw the car he said it wasn't a car. It was a large sneaker with a sensory environment to match.

She had the car for five days. Day One, the five 3D Jelly Belly air fresheners she purchased lent a saccharine air of a candy store to the interior of the coupé.

Day Two, she manually adjusted both outside mirrors to her satisfaction, after accepting that there was no automatic adjustment.

Day Three, the neighbor gave her a miniature sneaker to hang from the rearview mirror.

Day Four, as she was driving to work, she had a transforming moment. Her eyes widened. A smile spread across her face. Alone in that little lifesaver car, she started to laugh. She had begun to think about comparisons between Sneaker, as she had come to call the coupé, and herself. She had an epiphany of sorts. She realized she really related to the car.

She was little, measuring a mere five-foot-nothing barefooted, five-two in heels, which she detested wearing. She favored pink sneakers. Sneaker was quite little.

She was a useful member of society. She had a job. She paid taxes. Someday she would probably even schedule regular car checkups along with dental cleanings. Sneaker had certainly proven she was useful.

She had broken parts and working parts, as did Sneaker.

She was sometimes in need of airing out, but could be depended upon when really needed. Likewise Sneaker.

This was a deep and profound moment in her life. On Day Five, Hal, who knew he had passed off a loser car on her, was hard-pressed to understand why she actually patted Sneaker and smiled as she dropped her off at the end of the rental relationship.

"Just like the old days," Mr. D. remarked when I saw him a year later at Shoprite. "She's always surprised that my checkup-time call comes so fast. Same as you."

EARL'S STROKE

The real Earl and Margaret are role models for long-term commitment to each other and for keeping humor in their back pocket. Some of the details of stroke aftermath, determination, and recovery come from my mother, my brother-in-law, and my cousin Big Al.

When Margaret's husband, Earl, had his stroke, it changed his life and the lives of more people than we all first imagined. Of course it affected our Maggie. What would she do? Two of her three married kids were in Chicago and Indiana, so the grandkids only saw him twice a year on vacations. That wouldn't happen for a long time now.

More important for us, the weekly coffee club at Helene's would be out for Margaret. We didn't believe in book clubs. None of us retired teachers wanted to have another book assignment—too much like homework. We read enough on our own. Besides, talking about our kids, their kids, and their "issues," as they called them, was far more interesting and entertaining than any book on the bestseller list. Now Maggie was stuck with taking care of Earl.

Oh sure, her daughter, Sherry, helped. Sherry was the sterling daughter, always had been. In high school, Sherry had been in Honor Society, Young Nurses Club, was a candy striper, *and* she had a part-time job at Franco's Pizza. She never got in trouble and wasn't one of

105

those fast girls that got out of Catholic Academy and went wild in high school without all the nuns' rules echoing down the halls to keep them in line.

Most of us were dragged through the rebellious adolescence of our teenagers. One of the more worn-out mothers in our group at the time had just gone over to the high school for the fourth time for a conference about her son cutting classes. Over her *third* glass of wine she confided, "Just once, I wish Maggie would get some grief from Sherry. Even a minor smoking-in-the-bathroom infraction."

It never happened. Sherry graduated with honors, went to college, landed a great position where she gradually worked her way up to head of cardiovascular nursing at the University Hospital, married, and had kids. In that order. She and her husband bought a little handyman's special Cape Cod cottage in the next town, which was now impeccably decorated, and Sherry was currently president of the PTA.

Now that we were all grandmothers, we beamed with expectant pride knowing Sherry would do the right thing by her mom and dad's current difficulty. And she did. She went over to their house, did the grocery shopping when Maggie was at the hospital, and also visited her dad when he went to rehab.

But to be with Earl 24/7, that would be Maggie's challenge. Earl was a known curmudgeon and proud of it.

Much as Earl drove all of us nuts, we had to admit the biggest and saddest change was with Earl himself. No more singing Irish songs and jumping up and dancing at the community potluck dinners. His brain cells were on strike and not sending any mental commands to move, tap his foot, to talk and "raise just one more point, if I may."

Rehab and physical therapy three times a week helped wake up some of his brain cells that controlled locomotion. The cells gradually went back to work and started to send feeble messages to his muscles to shuffle his feet, raise his arms, and release his anger in words. At first, the words did not make sense, but the tone shouted "rage" at what had happened to him. For over two months he was bedridden and depressed.

His depression showed itself in anger and bitterness. He cursed at the nurses; he told Maggie he had nothing to live for. This after she drove over to the hospital on a snowy night with Eskimo Pie, expressly forbidden by the doctor. But he had wanted it, so Maggie went out and got it.

Don't think Maggie was a doormat. She took the bag of forbidden Eskimo Pie back very firmly, yet graciously, and turned to leave. "I guess I can find someone at the nurses' station who will force herself to eat this Eskimo Pie. Don't go away, Earl. I'll be right back." Margaret could deliver a reality check with style.

"No. Wait. Guess I eat."

She paused at the door with the bag raised in her hand. "To think your life could be given meaning by a frozen snack."

"Ah, Mags. Give me damn ice cream."

She walked back into the room, put the bag at the foot of the bed, still out of reach.

"Be nice to me, E. I am the best deal in town. Don't you forget it." She moved the bag to the tray table. As he took it, his hand lingered on hers.

Earl gradually reconciled to relearning all the basics of dressing himself, going to the bathroom, and brushing his teeth, but not without challenging the more inexperienced physical therapists with his moods. He was positively triumphant one day, beaming as Maggie walked into his room.

"By golly, beat my record today," he said, slapping his unaffected hand on the arm of the wheelchair. "Made little Serena cry in two minutes flat." Soon only the old guard nurses and therapists were sent to his room to reteach him to eat and walk.

"Don't mess with me, you old coot," Betty the battleaxe RN supervisor was heard to say. "I'm stronger than you, and I hold the key to the bathroom." She could fight fire with fire. "Besides, I know deep down you're just an old bear."

Somewhere into the sixth week of rehab, when he started moving his right leg on his own and could bend his right arm enough to feed himself, something else happened. This dour Irish man became an almost childlike and grateful seventy-five-year-old. He smiled at Betty. He patted Serena's hand when she gave him his meds.

When he was released from the acute care rehab and sent home, Maggie started operating the twenty-four-hour chauffer service. With the stroke Earl lost his balance, his mobility, his ability to make snap and concrete decisions, and so, lost his driver's license. No more quick trips to the VFW, which used to get him out of the house, giving him and Maggie each some breathing room.

She was on the caregiver road to burnout. The first time Maggie took Earl down to the VFW for the Monday gin game, he was welcomed like a returning hero. "I'll be back to get you at three o'clock," she said and made her escape home to two hours of blessed silence. You can imagine her surprise and small sparks of resentment when Earl stumbled into the house after forty-five minutes.

He slumped in the La-Z-Boy.

"What are you doing home?"

"Ken Murphy brought me." His face was white. "It was awful, Mags. My hands shook; I couldn't hold the cards still. I know there are shapes on the cards but those… those…"

"The suits?" she filled in.

"Yeah. Just meaningless blobs on the cards. When Pam, that volunteer, leaned over to me and said they were clubs or hearts or whatever, okay I took it. She's a nice girl, pretty too. But when she had to tell me those goddamn squiggles were numbers…" He stared at his Mags for rescue; she had none.

So no more trips to the VFW. No more reliving the foibles of his past and debating political candidates at every pre-primary luncheon and enumerating just what was wrong with this country. Earl had always had an opinion and never hesitated to share it with others. That his opinions were laced with negativity and narrow-mindedness was no deterrent to him.

After Earl had been home for four weeks, Maggie realized she needed to develop a bit of her own Betty Battleaxe attitude. Yes, her husband of fifty-five years had discovered his inner child, but he was still demanding.

"Mags, my love, I know you're busy, but could you put new batteries in the remote?"

"Maggie, me darlin,' what I wouldn't give for some of your homemade apple pie."

By the eighth week, when Margaret was about ready to pack her bags and move out, Earl got the medical clearance to go out for walks. The VFW was too far to walk and he refused to set up a taxi schedule with his fellow VFWers. Some of his curmudgeon habits were hardwired in him. Maggie had a schedule for what she called Mag's Mobile unit and refused to drive him when he got the whim. So where to walk? The mall, ah the mall, was only a ten-minute drive.

It turned out the local mall walkers club was a sanity-saving possibility. The main mall doors were unlocked at 7:00 AM expressly for The Club, as the walkers called themselves. This was before any stores opened or shoppers or hooky-playing teenagers began their daily pilgrimage. It was clean, level, and air-conditioned.

"Just what I want to do," Maggie told us at an abbreviated coffee meeting. "Look at clothes for size-zero women in store windows and hear screechy music wafting out of over-perfumed air from boutiques."

For seniors and those in physical rehab programs, the mall was safe terrain. A final bonus, the sponsoring hospital had a deal with Starbucks and Cinnabon—half price on the first round of coffee and buns. We were sure RN Sherry had a hand in that.

"Maggie, love, let's go down there," Earl cajoled. "We can walk. I can get my coffee. Bert Hobart," (a fellow VFW and unabashed curmudgeon), "goes every Tuesday and Friday."

Margaret was not moved by this talk of rehabilitative care.

Earl upped the ante. "I can walk and talk over old times with Bert. You can shop." He took Maggie's hand in his and gave it one of his newly discovered love pats. "I hear there's one of those scrapbooking stores there."

Now Margaret was a scrapbooking addict, with separate scrapbooks dedicated for each grandchild, their birth years, then school histories, and a scrapbook of each of the twice-yearly trips to Chicago and Indiana. And so the pact was made. Once around the mall, in and out of every nook and cranny, was a mile. Margaret met some of us at the food court or shopped and signed up for the scrapbooking workshops.

Earl and Bert joined The Club and proudly wore their Mall Walker tags around their necks, not only at the mall but also at Safeway, Home Depot, and yes, even to church. They walked, thrashing their way around the sofas, fountains, and kiosks. At first it was painfully slow. Their walkers were festooned with red, white, and blue ribbons and VFW patches. They graduated to three-pronged canes. Finally, they were on their own.

They may have lost some physical strength because of their strokes, but they lost none of their competitiveness. Soon Earl and Bert were in the Hundred-Miler Club, determined to log a hundred miles in the mall. "These youngsters, those ones with the seven earrings in one ear and their iPoops in the other, think they're hot stuff. We'll show them."

They were not above nudging slower walkers who did not heed their advance warning. "On your right. On your right. Madmen coming through." The only time the curmudgeon duo slowed down was to observe the younger female walkers in their Adidas walking shoes and pink Lycra capri pants with matching hot pink tops.

Earl regained an interest in life. He asked about the grandkids. He watched the news and ranted at the news commentators in his weakened stroke-affected voice. He regained an interest in physical fitness and the human anatomy, especially that of women.

When Bert went to Montreal to visit his daughter, Margaret got her own Mall Walker's Club tag and decided to join Earl in the walking. That's when she found out about the anatomy interest. She realized she had to steer Earl clear of the young women. He looked; he appreciated; and if he could, he reached out and touched. More than one young thing gave Earl a wide berth, but occasionally he hit home—right on the buttocks.

Margaret told this to Sherry over coffee while Earl wandered the food court after one of their Friday walks. "He'd be out with a pinch in the blink of an eye," she said. "It got so I had him hold the car keys in one hand. I held his other hand. Why, just this morning two lovelies went by and gave us a glance. 'Don't drop the keys,' I said to Earl and tightened my grip on his other hand."

Margaret fluttered her eyes and put her hand to her chest, getting ready for one of her dead-on imitations. "One of the lovelies gushed, 'How sweet. That old couple is holding hands while they walk.'"

You could hear Margaret's laugh clear across the food court. "'Oh, dearie,' I thought, 'if you only knew why.'"

BLOSSOMS

Some stories came my way bearing all their blossoms, fruits, or flowers. These are the full stories that needed only a bit of pruning and grooming. Many came from my personal journals, stories my husband and I have used to remind ourselves of shifts, growths, and new branches of our marriage. Others were delivered fully developed from cousins, parents, children, siblings, friends, and acquaintances.

Their stories are entertaining because the main characters not only enjoy life, but are also able to laugh at themselves.

In some of the blossom stories, the names have been changed, but the depiction of a father's love, infatuations, or lasting love and loyalty really happened to the main character.

IVAN AND THE FRENCH FRIES

The real Casey must be a teenager now. Her decision about French fries, told to me by her father, stayed with me and became this story used repeatedly as an example of family challenges and love. I added the details of the setting and other family history.

The kitchen clock read 11:30 AM

Casey was having one of those days. For an energetic three-year-old, this meant every toy was out of her toy box, she had already had two emotional meltdowns by lunchtime, and more food from her lunch bowl was in her hair than in her mouth.

Her mom, Teri, had just dashed out the door to her Saturday job down at the hardware store. Her flurry of kisses and "g'byes" lingered in the house along with the scent of Lily of the Valley. She had to be the only woman under the age of thirty-five who still wore Lily of the Valley.

Ivan was also having one of those days. For a thirty-five-year-old dad this meant he was late for the weekend job, his work gloves had disappeared into that black hole that also takes single socks and glasses, and he wasn't going to have *any* lunch.

He searched for the gloves while singing along with Casey. She was onto a new fingerplay song she had learned at preschool that required hand movements. "Open, shut them. Open, shut them."

115

She followed along behind him with her singsong voice. "Do it with me, Daddy. Do the hands too. I'll show you."

Before he knew it, the kitchen clock read 11:45. He had to punch in at noon.

Putting Casey in her booster chair, he reached for his jacket. When Casey saw him buttoning up his Andy's Automotive Supplies jacket, her eyes widened. Every time Daddy put on that shirt, he disappeared. "You stay here, Daddy." Casey's voice pierced his frantic search. "No work!"

He could tell by the pitch of her voice she was nearing another round of crying. *Where was that babysitter?*

"Oh, honey, I have to go," he soothed. "Here. Have some of your French fries."

"No!"

A French fry flew through the air and landed neatly near the ivy plant.

"Casey, Casey." Ivan crossed the six feet of the small kitchen and petted her curly brown hair as those big eyes looked up at him imploringly. He sat next to her chair and reached for another fry.

"Daddy, why do you go to work every day?"

Ivan leaned back in the chair, running a hand through his dark wavy hair. How to explain economics to a three-year-old? Bills to pay. A mortgage. The unexpected car repair. Raising a child meant expenses. More expenses than one salary could cover. But raising a child also meant storytelling, and singing songs, and fingerplays with hugs and kisses.

Casey was their first child. He could never fully describe the incredible pride he felt each Father's Day. His joy at this miracle he and Teri had created. His growing sense of accomplishment in his professional career. His confusion and frustration at being away from his family on weekends.

Things hadn't been easy in the last year. Oh, his career was taking off fine, but he was still at that entry level. This meant part-time work at the automotive store on Saturday and Sunday, then scrubbing with brown soap to get the oil and grease out for Monday morning at the accounting firm.

Casey was getting restless, calling, "Daddy Daddy Daddy" in that quick rat-a-tat cadence kids have.

"Daddy, why work?"

"Well, honey, I need to work to make money for our family."

"Why?"

"To pay bills." *No, that's wrong; she doesn't know what bills are.*

Casey slid down from her chair and crawled up on his lap. She laced her little fingers between his larger ones.

"What's bills?"

He cast about for a suitable explanation. *Try again, Dad.*

"Well," he said as he disentangled their hand connection and reached for the lunch, "to buy you French fries."

Casey looked up at her dad. She looked down at the French fries.

Her pudgy little hand reached out and slowly but firmly pushed the French fry dish as far away as her arm could reach.

"Okay, Daddy. No more French fries."

Casey sighed, a sweet contented sigh and leaned her head on his outstretched arm.

The clock ticked. 11:54.

KINDERGARTEN CUISINE—A THANKSGIVING MEMORY

True, all true! Mrs. Ball, the wonderful kids, my naïveté, and that little white stove that taught me about lots more than cooking.

"Is it ready yet?" a child's high-pitched voice asked. The room was filled with the delicious aroma of turkey. Nineteen mouths were waiting to be fed. Was it Grandma's house? No, it was my sunlit kindergarten classroom in New Jersey, the Tuesday before Thanksgiving.

When I was a young, single teacher, I was extremely dedicated to my job. I knew I made a positive difference in the lives of my young students. That November morning I was also suffering from one of those "I-said-I'm-gonna-do-it-and-by-golly-I'll-do-it" moments. In my personal life, I prided myself on cooking as little as possible. Strange to some, but to each his own. Pots and pans I had received as apartment gifts still nested in their boxes. My oven had that over-brilliant gleam only seen in new appliances. I had never, ever, cooked a turkey.

I was forced to re-examine my indifference to cooking when I changed my teaching assignment from third grade to kindergarten. I moved to Room 101, a spacious carpeted room with cozy reading area, sandbox area, and housekeeping corner complete with sink and a *real stove*!

The previous teacher had received an educational grant to purchase the stove for cooking. She had a positive zeal for multi-sensory learning. She did math lessons by baking brownies. Literature was a reading of *Stone Soup* and stirring up vegetable soup. Her classes finger-painted with chocolate pudding. Of course, her holiday feast of Pilgrims and Native Americans was topped off with the baking aromas of bread, or cookies, or cranberry or applesauce. Each November, aromas from Mrs. Ball's classroom drifted upward to the third-, fourth-, and fifth-grade rooms, producing a remarkable increase in volunteers to go help the kindergarteners.

When Mrs. Ball retired, I inherited her classroom. How could I not carry on this culinary tradition? I could do the brownies, pudding, and stone soup. But what could I do for Thanksgiving that was really special? Got it! I'd cook a Thanksgiving turkey. How hard could it be?

To simplify, I had precooked some stuffing the night before and crammed it inside any opening I could find in the turkey. The turkey was in the roasting pan when my munchkins entered the classroom.

"Look, there's our turkey. It looks funny!" High-pitched gobbles filled the classroom. Small bodies demonstrated a kindergartener's rendition of a turkey strut. We approached the stove, that sacred place where so many roasting pans and baking sheets had been placed in by loving hands and emerged bearing a tasty treat.

In went Little Tom, for he was just a four-pound turkey. He was big enough to carve a taste for each tiny mouth, yet small enough to cook in a half-day kindergarten session.

The wait was interminable. The Pilgrims donned their wide white paper collars and large, but lopsided, black paper hats. The Native Americans pulled on burlap vests, which I had whipped up on my old Singer sewing machine. I may have been a novice in the kitchen, but I knew my way around a sewing machine.

"My mother makes the best turkey," declared one outspoken Pilgrim.

"Who do you cook a turkey for if you live alone?" a young philosopher asked.

"How will we know when it's done?" queried another little one. Hey, I had done my homework. I knew about that little pop-up thermometer.

Near the end of our kindergarten morning, the moment arrived. Out he came from the oven. Oh, he looked beautiful. Golden brown and juicy. "Aahs" mixed with the aroma as Little Tom made his debut.

Now, to carve. I gave the blades of my never-been-used electric carving knife a test buzz. The children appreciated the drama of this.

Off came a diminutive drumstick. Zip! Off came the other one. Slicing down into the chest cavity, the blades snagged and stopped. Something glistened from the center.

What made me suddenly, but belatedly, think of it? Where were all the insides? Words like *gizzard, liver, heart* flashed though my brain. Anxiety gripped me. They were inside! The glistening was their wrapping. Paper wrapping—still inside.

Now when people are caught in an outright mistake, self-help books gently advise: Admit and accept mistakes. Laugh. Move on. However, it's much better to tell how you have accepted, laughed, and moved on after the fact, not while you are in it. Pride takes over when you are in it. Save face! Regroup! Think fast!

I diverted my students' attention by gesturing to our gaily decorated table. "Let's sit at the Thanksgiving table, my Pilgrims and Native Americans."

Their little heads turned, their bodies moved to the table, lured by the thought of actually munching turkey slices and downing apple cider.

Swiftly I got a death grip on the bit of paper poking through the chest cavity. With a twist and a tug, the bag of innards ejected with kind of long *ploppp!* I wrapped it in some paper towels.

"Well, my feasters, we're going to have white meat and dark meat. No stuffing today. That part of it just didn't work out."

Most of them accepted this, eagerly holding up paper plates

for their taste. All but my loyal Pilgrim, who looked at his meager offering and pronounced, "My mother still makes the best turkey."

Garden update: Mrs. B. tells me the stove was recently retired from the kindergarten room.

Shopping with Ellen

Intensity and an unbalanced power set-up typified this idolatry relationship. Gender and ethics faded to the background in this period of my adolescence. Names have been changed, but the actions, feelings, and the struggle for self-esteem disguised as having a best friend can be called up as if it were just the other day.

A soft musical sound and the smell of some kind of flowery stuff hit me as we went from the chill of a blustery March day into the warmth of the store. Unique Boutique is perfumed, unlike the pencil shavings and hotdog smell that wafted from Woolworth's, or pizza mixed with forbidden cigarette smoke at Frank's just up the avenue. This was important in the choice of stores.

Ellen's voice echoes in my head. "We're best friends, aren't we? We need to go shopping at a store that best friends would go to, not some junky five and dime."

I loved that—best friends. To be best friends with Ellen—Ellen of the beautiful clothes and dazzling smile encircling gorgeous white teeth, without braces. Boys left tokens of admiration on Ellen's desk— Bic pens, candy bars, records of the latest Chubbie Checker hit song. Nicky Talrest left a chocolate heart on her desk in homeroom, not even caring that his friends were all hooting and laughing at his adolescent crush. Ellen bestowed one of her smiles on Nicky, and then

122

split the whole box of candy with me at lunch even though Nicky was hanging around the cafeteria table waiting for one glance from her.

Now I feel Ellen nudging me from behind. "It's easy," she whispers. "Remember how easy it was at Woolworth's?"

I remembered—a lipstick slipped into my coat pocket as I walked by the waist-high counter. Wrigley's spearmint gum disappearing into Ellen's hand at the checkout counter as I fumbled for a dollar bill from my little purple plastic change purse to pay for my gum. Steal the lipstick, but pay for the gum. There seemed to be no rational thinking when I was with Ellen.

The first time I saw Ellen steal something, I was so shocked I gasped. She tilted her sweet face at the teenage counter boy, who happened to be Michael Corwin from our algebra class. Then she actually touched his arm with the hand that held the stolen gum— one finger pointed out and tapping his arm.

"Can you help me get that box of candy from that top shelf?" she asked. And she simply turned and winked at me.

Now "shopping" is an occasional part of our walk home from junior high. Today's store is definitely not Woolworth's. The addition of perfumed air and glass counters increases my paranoia that I'll get caught. I was almost laughing when we "shopped" in Woolworth's, but today my face feels hot and my hands are clammy and cold.

My friend Ellen is flawlessly beautiful. No limp hair or problem teenage skin for her. Her dark hair falls in shiny waves down her back. Her eyes are actually green with little bits of gold in the iris when you get up real close and look. I know because I've been that close.

I was as taken with Ellen's teenage charm as the boys in algebra class. I was so envious of her beauty, her clothes, and her seeming careless confidence that I brushed aside her stealing as easily as flicking crumbs off a table.

Last Tuesday we walked to her house after school. Her mom works at the insurance building in town so the house was completely ours. What a feeling of freedom for two fifteen-year-old girls testing the boundaries of adult rules. After we had a cup of coffee and smoked two forbidden cigarettes—ironically my first coffee but not my first cigarette—we moved to the bathroom, where Ellen's mother kept all her makeup. Ellen's house was the first house I had been in that had two sinks in the bathroom. This one was littered with lipsticks, mascara, powdered eye shadow, and foundation cream. I was mostly interested in doing something to make my plain brown, sparsely lashed eyes look alluring.

"My eyes are okay," Ellen remarked, as she shifted toward me and looked at herself sort of sideways in the mirror.

"Look," she said. "My mother says there are golden flecks. Are they really there?"

That's when she turned full-face to me for the examination. To have Ellen's gold-flecked green eyes staring at me was overpowering. It took my breath away. A comment from me was neither forthcoming nor necessary. I knew that she knew the flecks were there. Ellen liked to be looked at. She had learned a long time ago that reactions to her looks would always be positive.

But now at the Unique Boutique those green eyes are watching me. "Go," her voice hisses. "Do it."

A pale saleswoman with her hair in a Grace Kelly French twist glides over to us.

"Um, can I see that silky scarf over there?" asks Ellen.

The saleslady keeps pace behind the counter as Ellen trails her hand along the glass case to the far end of the displays.

I step back into the aisle. There are no other customers in the store, but it's also a very small space. Only three short aisles across the center and a long accessory counter on the side for perfume, jewelry, scarves, and gloves. And huge mirrors I hadn't noticed until now. Those mirrors will reflect every tiny movement.

I didn't even think of arguing to forgo shopping at all. I had argued for the boutique over the jewelry store in town because Mr. Salter owned the jewelry store. Mr. Salter is a pale, quiet man whose shoulders are in an eternal slump from having to provide for three kids, a wife, a dog, and a mangy cat. The Salters also live on my street at the end of town. Shopping at his store is far too risky. I can't steal from someone I actually know. That would be immoral.

"It has to be big," were my beautiful instructor's words. "What's the use of trying at the boutique unless it's really expensive and a challenge?"

I touch the thin gold bracelet on my right wrist. A souvenir from our visit two weeks ago that Ellen has convinced me to wear today.

I had tried unsuccessfully to hide it in my pocket as we walked through town. "But they'll know it's from their store and I didn't buy it."

Ellen delivered a kind of pep talk as we got nearer to Unique Boutique.

"Dum dum, don't you remember your boyfriend gave it to you?" She put her arm around my shoulders, rocking me gently but steadily. "Now practice saying that."

Her lips moved silently as I said, "Oh, this? You have this same bracelet? My boyfriend gave me this for Valentine's Day." I exhaled.

"Again."

I said it so many times I almost believed I had a boyfriend, and one who would have money to buy a gold bracelet for me. Such was the weight of my crush on Ellen and the power of her words over me.

"Too easy for our shopping today," Ellen has said of the bracelet. "No more little stuff."

My book bag is a wide canvas tote. Today it is purposely empty of books. My heart is pounding. I'm sure the saleslady will hear it and look up at just the wrong time. My hands are so sweaty. I know they'll leave handprints on the glass case, an instant clue when the police come later to investigate this crime.

I turn into the aisle. Puffy wool sweaters are folded on glass shelves—small, medium, and large. Top, middle, and bottom shelves. Opening the clasp on my book bag with one hand, I scoop a big-buttoned pink cardigan into the bag. I close the flap with shaking fingers, sling the bag over my shoulder, and sidle up next to Ellen. I feel perspiration dripping down the sides of my arms. I can't look to see if it shows. I stare at Ellen. *Let's go. Let's get out of here.*

She's got the scarf up by her neck and is looking at herself in the mirror. Her porcelain skin is so white. You can see blue veins in her neck. Her green eyes squint just a little. I think she does this for effect because it makes her long eyelashes flutter.

"Oh, I like it," she coos.

"Shall I wrap it for you, dear?"

"No, I'll wear it."

Ellen takes out the two twenties lifted from her mother's purse that morning, slides them all crumpled over the counter, gets her change, and beams angelically at the saleslady. The woman smiles back in a kindly way. I want to leave. Ellen stops to lean over the counter to look at another scarf. *No, no, I want to get out of here.* Ellen hooks her arm through mine and pulls me away as if I were the casual customer. We turn to leave.

"Oh, dear?" The saleswoman's cool voice has risen in volume.

I freeze. I look at Ellen without turning my head. Ellen turns back to her. "Yes?"

"Don't you want the receipt?"

"Oh, yes. Thank you," says Ellen. "My mom will want it." Ellen and I know it's to use when Ellen returns the scarf on Saturday when another saleslady is on.

"Thanks. Bye."

"Bye-bye now, girls."

Each step away from Unique Boutique is harder because I think it's the step where I will get called back again. Called and caught. Then flung into jail to experience the dire consequences of my escalating shoplifting career. No one will call me "dear" then.

But no one calls me. The sun is shining. It's a beautiful late-winter afternoon. We're at the last few blocks of our walk home from school.

By the time we reach the railroad tracks, I've flimsily revised my future. I'm fifteen and free. I got away with it. My pounding heart is replaced with a feeling of triumph, almost smugness. Who needs rules? Who needs those stupid babysitting jobs to buy extra clothes and jewelry? This is the way to go! Our laughter surrounds us as we walk home.

Adults passing by smile at the two happy teenage girls hugging each other as they go their separate ways at the end of a carefree school day. Lucky girls, this is the best time of their lives.

"Bye, toots," Ellen calls as she makes the left turn onto her street. "See you tomorrow."

"Same time. Same place."

I never wore the pink sweater.

BE PREPARED

I wish we knew the real Tony and Pam's names and their background. But the rest of this—all true. This complete story is still a favorite with my sister and me. I hope it becomes a favorite for you too.

The highlight of our summer vacation at Brant Lake in the Adirondack Mountains of New York is always the first boat ride. My brother-in-law, Paul, having had some experience on water, is the captain of our crew and so wears a jaunty captain's hat. My sister, Eileen, packs a picnic lunch for the requisite stop on the deserted island in the middle of the lake. I pack a bag with our supply of sunblock, magazines, and binoculars to spy on the large stately homes still termed "summer cottages" and "camps." My husband, Hank, provides the services of captain's mate for our maritime adventure.

Brant Lake is tiny by Adirondack native standards. This lowers the ranking of the lake in the eyes of more aggressive boaters who require hours of lake exploring, or those who want some current or waves that can be found on the larger thirty-two-mile Lake George. Brant Lake's six-mile length is twice the width of Lake George. Just right for us.

This vacation lake is synonymous with paradise. For a glorious week each summer the four of us rented the same lakefront cottage nestled in the woods. The house was built around the huge living room with its stone fireplace, floor-to-ceiling built-in bookshelves laden with all the old books your mother and father grew up on, even an old yellowed Boy Scout manual emblazoned with the motto "Be Prepared." The screened-in porch barely protected the old wicker furniture and a solid oak dining table that today would cost thousands of dollars in any New York City antique store.

Our third season on the lake started out the same as the second and first—on a brilliant, blue sky summer day. Earlier that Saturday, my husband and I had arrived around 10:00 AM, traveling the 230 miles from New Jersey in under four and a half hours. "A record," Hank announced, thumping his hand on the steering wheel as we pulled up to the cabin. The musty closed-up-all-winter smell permeated the "cottage." I started opening and propping up windows with makeshift wedges. At the kitchen window, I stopped to lean on the windowsill to admire a young monarch butterfly, perhaps enjoying his summer vacation before beginning his three-thousand-mile flight to Mexico.

"They're here," I shout to Hank as I see Eileen's VW pull around the curve of the widened dirt path that passes for a driveway. "Come on. Come on."

"I'm coming. Jeez, I thought you wanted me to bring everything in and unpack."

"Leave it. They're here." I'm out the back door, which I guess is really the front door. How do people decide front and back when the house faces the lake?

Eileen pulls up to the edge of the grass and I hear the rumble of Paul's motorcycle before I see him bumping along the driveway. They've traveled like this each time we've vacationed in the Adirondacks. "How could I travel along these great roads and leave the bike at home?" is Paul's thinking. It's a no-brainer for Paul, who has been riding since he was a teenager.

So Eileen brings boxes of food and clothes in the car up the New York Thruway and Northway while Paul winds his way up the back roads.

"How is it? How does it look?" she calls from the car.

"Everything is exactly the same."

"Great. Mmm, I can smell the woods," she says into my hug. She hands me her quilted bag that I know holds her latest sewing project. Hank pulls a double pack of juice from the car, and she grabs a tote.

Paul is taking off his helmet to reveal his happy smile as he and Hank shake hands and hug around the juice bottles. We make several trips from car to house as tennis rackets, beach blankets, and floats are stowed away.

"We're heeere," we all shout.

"I made chicken for tonight so no cooking necessary," I tell my sister as we put food into the tiny refrigerator.

"Great! I brought a salad from home and made brownies at six this morning."

Eileen squeezes my arm. "You know, even with all the windows open, that musty smell is still in the air. It means country to me."

Once everything is away, and we've put shorts and T-shirts over bathing suits, it's time for the opening ceremony of vacation—going for the first boat ride. Alongside the narrow beach is a rickety old wooden dock leading out to the boat. The boat is a sixteen-foot aluminum rowboat tied up at the edge of the dock. Called simply Boat, it was painted green, had two old rusty oarlocks, even older wooden oars, and a fifteen-horsepower motor. Small, but sufficient to putt up and down the length of the six-mile lake.

"Let's go, let's go." We pile in with bug spray, picnic tote, and magazines. Off we go. Cap'n Paul at the helm, Eileen at the fore, face into the breeze, Hank and I in the middle. The boat pulls away from the dock, bouncing just a bit over the choppy waves and sending up spray as we hit the wake of other boats. It's a grand day and our hearts are singing along with the hum of the motor.

Our song is short-lived once we reach just about the center of the lake. The motor emits sort of a gradual gurgling song, then a buzz, then silence. The only sound is water lapping against the gently rocking Boat.

Paul pulls on the starter cord. Nothing. Again he pulls with some vocal accompaniment, not complimentary to the working of the boat. Eileen asks in a joking manner, "Did you check the gas?"

Now when people are thrust into a situation that contains the components for embarrassment or blame placement, they utilize various defense mechanisms to deflect or lessen the effects of such blame on themselves. Research shows that group dynamics affect which defense is chosen. Husbands and wives usually blend as one to support each other in a larger group setting where there is conflict.

I think this also holds true in less legally binding partnerships. In my younger and less stable years, I myself would capriciously instigate jealous tension at local festivities if my date was flirting with someone. In being told to "tone it down," we would unite with each other and often escalate the tension by turning against the object of the flirtation. This often resulted in our being invited to leave, which was guaranteed to bond us together as we exited. I must add that alcohol was usually involved. But that was so long ago.

Now, as part of a long-married couple, I know my beloved's habits as well as the habits of my sister and her husband. After ten years of the four of us traveling together, when such a blame situation arises, we fall back into not partnership groupings, but traditional gender segregation and splits. Also Eileen is my sister. My twin sister. So I guess it could be the old "blood is thicker than water" mechanism at work, a tie as primordial as you can get. But by gender grouping, the playing field is leveled somewhat for Hank and Paul.

So in the case of the no-gas dilemma, this means Paul and Hank gaze at each other in a sort of visual bonding that seems to communicate, "What do we say about this?" No answer is necessary because they both appropriate a slack-jawed blank look.

Eileen and I, wanting to avoid the blame target, join the gender game. Eileen exchanges humor for serious, and unlike her, sexist chore delineation. "It is the man's job to check the reliability and readiness of the traveling vehicle. Were it a canoe, it would be the male job to make sure the paddles were in the canoe."

I back her up, directing my remark to Hank. "If we were hiking, you'd make sure the backpack had the map." This has all been programmed in us from birth. However, we also know feminism is a situational ethic. Intellectually we know better. Fuel is nongender. But when your back's to the wall, you resort to old ways.

Pride is now involved, so it becomes the male job to supply the solution to the no-gas problem.

Cap'n Paul declares, "We'll row to the lake's end and get gas down at the boat station."

"We'll take turns rowing," adds Hank.

"Good." My sister and I smirk. And we "gals" settle back to get the sun.

After some changing of positions, Paul is in center to row, I am back at the rudder, Eileen still up front, and Hank at the ready for the second rowing shift.

Some time into Hank's rowing shift, we are not much closer to the gas pump but are nearer to lakeside than lake center. The lake, deciding to test our coping abilities still further, turns against us and snaps at the left oar, breaking it, leaving a small chunk of oar in Hank's hand while the bulk of it floats away.

No gas, one oar. Admit defeat? Never! This is still a gender/ pride and now man-against-the-elements conflict. "We'll do it with one oar," Paul boasts.

The only thing done with the one-oar technique is to create a circular movement and a small whirlpool.

"We need to get help," Eileen ventures to suggest.

"We'll call to the next boat and ask them to help us."

"Yes! Yes." Now we are all united in this effort.

In the distance the sound of a motor is heard. A snappy speedboat approaches holding two couples. They are tan, healthy, young, and virile looking. Their laughter floats above the sound of the motor. What makes us lose our collective voice to call out? Could it be age embarrassment? Our collective life experience is about a hundred and eighty years. We should know the ropes, so to speak. Our chance glides by. We slump.

Hank uses his managerial skills. "Next boat, we're all going to shout. I'll count 'one, two, three.'"

Again "Yes! Yes!" We rally. Together we'll get through this.

Again in the distance comes the sound of a motor. Was it a speedboat? A sailboat? Who knows? Hank's "one, two, three" was followed by a weak "Halloo! Help us." Oh, weaklings! Mewling kittens!

Before we can recover from this humiliation, the mocking sound of a motor comes up from behind us. Hank's eyes are glazed. Eileen is hunched, at a loss. Paul is audibly cursing the boat, the oar company, and the Adirondack Forest Rangers.

From somewhere deep within me comes this voice. I stand. The spirit of the Unsinkable Molly Brown is made flesh. "Hey, we need help. Hel- help." I wave my arms. I shout and, lo and behold, a speedboat veers toward us. It is a purple fiberglass with specks of glitter speedboat with a tinted windshield. A small flag with a six-pack graphic on it flutters off the back.

Our saviors are an older couple, faces tanned and weather-lined from more than three seasons on the lake.

He speaks. "You folks need help." It is neither a question nor a condescending indictment as he pulls alongside and extends his hand to Hank. "Tony Biondo. This is Pam." He pushes his cap back on his head. "New up here, eh?"

"Uh, yeah. Could you pull us to the gas station?"

"I didn't think I'd seen you before. I know that boat. Can't place the cabin it goes with though." He puts a dark square hand on Boat's rim to keep us in this holding pattern. "We retired up here twelve years ago and I know every house and family on this lake." He's settling in for a lake resident talk. Year-rounders have all the time in the world and never settle for straight information or action when a good long visit will do just as well.

Pam nudges Tony. "T, they need help."

He gives her a kiss on the cheek. "You're right, chickie." And turns to us. "Gas station's closed. But no problem," says our rescue boat captain. "We'll take you to your cottage." I get the feeling that Tony has done this before. "Where're you staying?"

"Oh, down at the end a ways."

"Well, we'd better get started then, hadn't we?" Tony's captain's hat has a black vinyl brim almost as sparkly as his mirrored sunglasses, which thankfully hide whatever pitying look he has in his eyes.

He hooks a rope to our prow and we ride off, faster than Boat could have gone under its own steam.

There's no way this can look like it is a planned outing. Pam turns around as one house after another appears around each cove and mouths, "Is this it?" as she points hopefully toward shore.

We gesture, "No, down farther." She half smiles and leans over, relays the message to Tony, who waves a hand overhead in what I can only hope means "No problem." On we go.

Yes, we get back to the cottage. We stand like four orphaned kids as Tony and Pam zoom off into the late-day sun. It is a silent, yet wiser, group that wends its way up the path and onto the porch. Eileen takes the lunch bag into the kitchen and comes back with a pitcher of iced tea and four glasses. As she pours, she announces, "To our survival."

She tosses the yellowed Boy Scout manual on the porch table.

Hank reaches across and picks it up. "I know just what this needs." He gets a pencil stub and writes, "Check the gas" across the top. A small smile finds its way across his face.

"You know, that whole boat ride will make a pretty good story at Jack's Grill tonight when one of the locals asks Tony, 'Anything interesting happen at the lake today?'"

"Not much," I say in my best imitation of Tony's kindly voice. "Just another group of summer folks who went astray."

THE HEEL

In the early years of my second marriage, Hank and I discovered, to our surprise, annoyance, and sometimes embarrassment, that we had some vastly different ideas about what was right, or romantic, or even fair. I felt confident in this marriage, recalling the thousands of dollars I had invested in self-actualization (my lofty description of years of therapy). I had gone on to professional family dynamics training, which stressed active listening whereby one spoke gently during, shall we say, discussions with the possibility of tension, i.e., "What I hear you saying is you do not want to continue our weekly dance lessons that I have enjoyed beyond belief."

In spite of this academic and therapeutic background, I sometimes, oh all right, very frequently smashed up against the wall of self-centeredness and was forced to crawl through the door of humility into the land of awareness and back into the cozy glow of our togetherness.

To keep us from repeating mistakes of past relationships or our family of origin in this bright and shiny new marriage, our conversations were along the lines of, "We are the architects of our relationship; we are not copying the blueprint of another." "Yes, we can take what we like of some and leave the rest."

An example of how this works please, you ask. Since you are reading this and cannot see my blush of embarrassment, I will share.

But first some background, sometimes known as righteous justification:

My favorite meal is a scrumptious and luxurious breakfast. Is it a reaction to my childhood breakfasts, which were planned first and foremost with nutrition in mind—starting with a soft-boiled egg? How can anyone like soft-boiled eggs? Runny, mushy with the yolk sometimes still semi-translucent? My sisters and I were served one soft-boiled egg, one piece of whole wheat toast with a brief swipe of the knife that had barely kissed the margarine. This was accompanied by freshly squeezed orange juice and a small alphabet of vitamins—B, C, and E. The torture of chewing on dry toast was multiplied when you got the last piece of bread at the end the loaf, which was the dreaded heel.

The heel, as most people know, is almost all crust. It is not as soft, not as comforting to eat, and therefore almost universally despised. Sometimes by the time one gets to the heel, the bread has aged and is less than fresh, so it has hardened a bit, and the heel side is even tougher.

I can still recite my mother's rationalization: "It's still good for you. We're not going to waste food. Eat it." We ate briskly and in an atmosphere of what can only be described as utilitarian dining. Food on plate, with utensils, glass, and napkin on the oilcloth tablecloth that served as our breakfast, lunch, and dinner table cover. Sit, eat, swallow vitamins, clear dishes, leave table.

During my years at college, I discovered new modes of meal serving and dining. College cafeteria food was not inspiring, although there was certainly an abundance of food. No limits on the number of times you could go through the line with your plate piled high. I discovered I loved toast with butter, real butter, and jam. Even in college, the heels of the loaves of bread were passed over on the bread trays and abandoned like so many orphans.

It was before my 8:00 AM Spanish class that my love affair with breakfast began. I liked piles of bacon. I loved pancakes smeared with syrup. You're cringing at the caloric intake? Come on, I was eighteen, had a teenager's metabolism, worked out in the gym, and dripped with sweat in the dance studio with a group of other aspiring dancers.

You can well imagine my burgeoning gluttony when I discovered the world of eating outside my home and beyond the college campus. In college this meant diners! If you have not lived in New York or New Jersey, you don't understand. New Jersey diners do not have servers. They have waiters and waitresses. They don't tell you they are your server. You know it immediately. They "coffee you up" while you are still saying, "Yes, I'll have coffee." The waitress has a coffeepot permanently affixed to her pouring hand, deftly refilling as she goes by your booth with another order.

And the bread! Rye, wheat, sourdough, challah, pumpernickel, and white. Toast, bagels, grilled cheese sandwiches, three-decker clubs, French toast, with never a heel to be seen.

Fast forward to the year Hank and I got married. We were on a pretty strict budget. He had divorce payments, we had two teenagers, and we were saving to buy a house. We rarely went out to eat. My answer to "What do you want for your birthday?" was "I'd like breakfast in bed."

Hank was inspired. The first B in B, as we came to call this presentation, was brought in on a white wicker tray with *The New York Times* in the side pocket, a tall glass of OJ, two eggs over easy, two slices of rye toast slathered with butter and cut on the diagonal, which is always so much better than cut into two rectangles. The presentation included using the good silverware with a linen napkin folded on the side. My saliva glands stirred, the taste buds on my tongue perked up. This was living. This was a gift from a loving husband.

A bite of egg, a sip of juice, and then, the climax—to bite into the toast. My hand froze. I think I physically recoiled. The toast was… the heel. Was that the last of the loaf of bread? Was he being funny?

My sweetie was waiting expectantly. I spoke from love. "It's wonderful. Thank you."

Such was the success of this breakfast, that two months later, on Mother's Day, the wicker tray made an encore appearance—scrambled eggs, very crisp bacon, cranberry juice, and a rose in a tiny acrylic bud vase that had LOVE etched into it. My eyes scanned to the bread first. I couldn't help it. I poked at it with my index finger. Again... the heel. *Come on.* I felt my face get hot.

"Eth, what is it? What's wrong?"

One of the things we had agreed on in our recent communication clarifications was that the response was never to be "Nothing" to the question "What's wrong?" when in fact, something was wrong.

I was possessed with the perceived deprivation of childhood. "Why did you give me the heel? What kind of present is that? To give me the heel."

Hank's mouth went into that O of genuine astonishment. He had no response.

Ha! See, he is being mean. My actualized adult Ethel vanished. The petulant child in me took over. I believe the look on my face could be labeled a pout.

Hank turned and left the room. I almost cried. *So much for talking things out.* When he returned he had the remaining loaf of bread in his hand. The package was not empty, there were about six pieces left. *So why'd he give me the heel?*

"Let me tell you something," he began as he sat on the side of the bed. "I wanted to give you a really special breakfast in bed. So I fixed all this and deliberately gave you the heel. When I was growing up, whoever my mother gave the heel to was the special one for the day and sure to have good luck. It got so when someone got the heel, my sisters would say, 'Oh, you're the special one.' So, honey, you're the special one."

The heel of my childhood or the heel of his? We kept the one from his.

Garden Harvest: Knowing the symbolism of the heel that we adopted, I can sometimes take it without hesitation. I wrote this as a reminder for me. "It's a heel thing" is a phrase that reduces tension in our house.

AUTOMOTIVE ADVENTURES

The true vignettes of my mother's driving experiences came together into this blossom story that tells about changes, both in her actions and life perspective.

People do change after they retire. When my parents retired, the biggest change was their move from our Long Island New York suburban house to a smaller home in the lazy town of Tryon, North Carolina. Life slowed down. Both my parents got a little smaller. Mom measured four-foot-eleven and was shrinking, weighing in at just around a hundred pounds. After my father died, Mom became more independent, of necessity.

By the time she was eighty-two, my mother was completely white-haired. Some would say she was a tiny woman. My dad taught her to drive when they were in their teens and courting. So she'd been on the road for about sixty-five years. She put a lot of mileage on her cars. But I noticed a new change while she was driving her '98 dark green Toyota Corolla.

I would say my mother had always been a cautious, serious driver. She looked both ways, observed all the laws, and boasted of her unblemished driving record. Still had the clean driving record too, though not as pure as the driven snow.

She customized the driver's seat of the Toyota with a pillow for her back and one to boost her height. I noticed this new quirk when

Mother got around automobiles whether she was the passenger, the driver, or riding shotgun. There was an almost imperceptible increase in her spirit of adventure derived from her driving experiences.

Her caution became tempered with a certain boldness when she was in the driver's seat. She began accelerating in thirty-mph zones.

There was also a gaiety and lightheartedness when she was the passenger. As she said, "There's not a whole lot to do here in the backseat." This previously silent traffic watcher began chattering about local gossip or town landmarks we passed.

Where she used to pay attention to details while riding shotgun and was quite adept at giving directions, she developed a new cavalier, laissez-faire attitude.

Along with her attitude, I realized just how small and lightweight my mother had become when we were driving home from the airport at the beginning of her Thanksgiving visit with us in New Jersey. She was in the backseat behind me, telling us about her cat, her neighbors, and the local gossip. My husband, Hank, took a rather sharp corner turn. Mom's conversation was cut short with a gasp. I turned to see her slide across the seat from left to right and disappear from view. All we heard was her laughter as she lay prone on the seat. Hank's take on it in the rearview mirror was a "Now you see her, now you don't."

The laissez-faire attitude was further demonstrated as we drove from our house to the airport at the close of the Thanksgiving visit. My husband was taking a new shortcut and we—dare I say this?—got lost. He was using the "drive and turn, don't stop to ask for directions" method even though we had passed several gas stations. I knew there was a limited amount of time to reach the airport for the flight departure.

When I remarked on this, my mother's response was, "Oh, no problem, I like driving around. If I miss my flight, I'll just come back and stay with you a few more days."

My darling spouse pulled into a gas station faster than you could say "house guest."

Mom's adventurous reputation was enhanced as she related a

Driving Miss Daisy mishap she had with her rock garden. "I just misjudged it slightly, but the gardener says you won't even be able to tell where I went over the gladiolas."

And the unblemished record was slightly marred with her confession of a driving warning after being stopped by a local traffic cop. "They sure are young," was her not-so-innocent observation.

But he knew how to handle her. "License and registration, ma'am. Now, ma'am, y'all got to watch out for these older folks who come out of that Tryon Estates retirement complex. You know some of 'em don't even look, or stop, or signal. And quite a few of 'em got a heavy foot."

"Was I going really fast, officer?"

"You were barreling, ma'am. I'm presentin' you with a warning this time. Y'all slow down, hear?"

She had never gotten pulled over before. She had never had a ticket or even a warning, and the look on her face as she retold this episode signaled her remorse at this threat of change in her official driving reputation. The warning slip was tucked in the glove compartment as a reminder of her run-in with the law. But it did not remain an orphan for long. On my next visit there were six warnings lined up along the frame of the dining room mirror. Not hidden. And waved at in a way that was both dismissive and held a hint of pride.

"Gee, Mom, good thing you didn't buy a red Toyota. You know they call them speeding-ticket red."

"Well," she sniffed, "my little green car will do for now."

As she was pulling out of a parking space later that day, her eyes lit up when I remarked, "Hey, you could get yourself something like that white Mustang convertible there."

She stopped—in the middle of the road—to gaze at it and replied smoothly, "I think I'd like it in red."

DANCING WITH MY MOTHER

A fully grown story that I cherish more each year. My time with my mother in the last five years of her life was the jewel in the crown of our relationship. Mom had the same birthday conversation with each of her daughters, not remembering her age, and being equally delighted each time she heard us tell her. Who says repetition is boring?

So what will it be today? This was the question I asked myself as I strode down the hallway of the Regent Nursing Residence to visit my eighty-eight-year-old mother. My mother was declining, both physically and emotionally. A hemorrhagic stroke three years earlier had robbed her of any thought of independent living. Her retirement home with its well-tended gardens, indoor plants, and tiny art studio adjacent to the washer and dryer on the lower level had been sold.

The stroke robbed her of right-sided movement, coordination to hold a paintbrush, and concentration for staying focused. Her activities were limited to wheelchair movement within the boundaries of the nursing home. Her patience and tolerance, never her strong points, were greatly reduced.

She was a true regent mother, garnering a private room with her own needlepoint armchair, drop-leaf table, and oil paintings from her dabbling in landscape and still life art. Most of the other residents shared both a room and institutional furniture. Mother thought the private room was only her due.

Although she spoke slower than before the stroke, she still remained strongly opinionated and curious. So each day's visit was a toss of the coin as to which Mom persona would be sitting in her wheelchair in Room 104. If the blinds were open and her favorite big band CD was playing, I'd visit with the childlike Excited Mom who was a delightful and sometimes outrageous companion. "I have a great idea for Halloween. Next week. Bring my old bathing suit from the 1930s. The one I used to wear to costume parties. Liven things up around here."

Or my mother's body could be inhabited by what I called the Dark Force. Then the blinds would be closed, no light, no music. "Get me out of here," she'd rasp. "They're trying to kill me with boredom. Who wants to watch those ninnies on the soaps? They can never figure out the men are incorrigible rakes."

Today the door was partly open. I arranged my smile and walked in. Blinds were open. Good sign. But no music. Not a good sign. Mom looked up from the picture album on her lap. She beckoned me with one curled finger, a terrific scowl on her face and brown eyes widened. "Come here," she whispered. It was a Dark Force day.

"Hi, Mom." I bent to give her a kiss. Her hand stopped me less than five inches from her face.

"This place is filled with old people."

"Yes?"

"This is a mistake. I don't belong here. They're all old and crotchety."

I know it's hard to believe, but I was relieved to hear this. My sisters and I weren't sure if my mother was aware of her surroundings in the nursing home. She went to Bingo and played Trivial Pursuit in the activity room with other residents. But she had never asked about where she was.

Prior to the stroke, she had had almost weekly rants about the senior drivers in her town. "They drive like snails. Not the young ones. The ones with white hair. Those old people shouldn't be on the road." It was then an inner struggle to refrain from pointing out that she herself had more than a nodding acquaintance with the local traffic cop. Remember her warning tickets for speeding? The six of them lined up along the mirror frame in her dining room had been like old dance programs she had kept as a teenager. To hear her pick up a familiar thread of complaining was oddly comforting.

"Yes, Mom, most people are here because they got hurt or got too old and could not take care of themselves in their houses anymore. You had your stroke and now you have someone feed you and bathe you here because you could not do that at home. You have the doctor and nurses right here to give you your pills and check your heart."

"Yes, yes, they're okay. But the ones in the big room. Ethel, they're all old ladies." She curled herself even smaller in her chair and dropped her head in an exaggerated geriatric droop.

"Well, even though they are so old, isn't there anyone here that you really like?"

My mom was no fool. She had some choices here. She could be really contentious and say she hated everyone or she could pick the most unlikely candidate just to play devil's advocate. She knew how to keep things lively.

"I like Helen." Helen was the ninety-four-year-old female terror of Regent House. Where my sisters and I had nicknamed the female residents The Regents, Helen could easily qualify as the Wicked Queen. Her daily conversation was more than sprinkled with swear words. I think my mother was secretly envious of Helen's freedom of speech. Helen had claimed a private table by the main column in the dining room, while other residents sat four to a table. No one objected to this because no one wanted to sit with her anyway. For some reason Helen had taken a liking to my mother and requested that Mom sit at her table. She would exhort my mother, who could only swallow pureed foods, to eat up.

"Gladys, you eat like a bird. What's this crap they're feeding you anyway?" She had to be stopped from putting biscuits and chicken wings on my mother's plate. She snuck contraband chocolate chip cookies into the bag on my mother's wheelchair, which my mother took back to her room and dipped in water until they were soggy enough to swallow. Socially, it was a good match. Helen talked up a storm and my mother's speech was slow and hesitant. Mom seemed quite comfortable with the eating and entertainment arrangement with Helen in charge.

Thinking of something to report about her day that also contained some shock value gave my mom a conversation opener. "Helen said a naughty word this morning at breakfast. The aide wanted her to apologize for saying it in front of me, but I told her it didn't bother me at all."

I didn't bite at the bait to get into a game of Guess the Swear Word whereby I would have to recite all the four-letter words I could think of thereby titillating my mother's sense of racy living along with giving her the opportunity to play chastising mother at my speech. I saw a way to make my point about the median population at her residence. "Well, you know, Helen is in her nineties, Mom. Wouldn't you say that's old? She fits into the old lady category and you like her."

"That's Helen." Mom dismissed my argument with a wave of her unimpaired hand. "She's different. But the rest of them. Old nincompoops."

I tried again. This was a possible segue into the conversation I wanted to have with Mom. Not a perfect segue, but you have to take the opportunity when it comes.

"Mom, your birthday is next week. Your other darling daughters will be here. I can bring a big cake for the residents."

"Those biddies? Bah!"

"How about candy for the staff? We'll have a celebration. Sing some songs. Talk about some of the exciting things you've done in your life." I tapped the photo album from her trip with my father to Paris in the 1970s.

"What do you mean celebrate? Can't move anymore. Can't paint. Can't write."

I persisted in laying the groundwork for the birthday celebration. "I'll bring balloons. You'll get to wear the birthday tiara." This was a silvery crown polished up for each birthday girl in our family. "We'll play 'Moonlight Serenade' and you can tell us about you and Dad dancing." My mother and father had been reigning dance champions in our family. They danced at home in the kitchen. Or Dad would lead Mom in a smooth fox trot on the porch on summer nights. Even into their late seventies, they went square dancing once a week. Their biggest claim to fame, albeit in a dance group, was dancing at the 1965 World's Fair in New York.

"Can't dance." She attempted a celebration block.

"You and I will dance," I countered.

Mom hit the arm of the wheelchair with her left hand. "In this?"

"Yes." I was not my mother's daughter for nothing. I took a risk. I reached over and clicked on the CD player. Sounds of Glenn Miller began to fill the room. I reached down and released the brake on the wheelchair. My mother's gaze followed my hand. The next few minutes were carried out in slow motion.

I lifted the photo album and put it on the bed. I stood up, reached out on either side of the wheelchair, and turned it to face me. Standing in front of my mother, I waited while she raised her eyes to look at my face. I raised my right hand, palm open, an invitation to the dance.

"Remember, Mom?"

My mother looked at my hand, slowly lifted her trembling left hand, and placed it in mine. I started to sway side to side. She mimicked my movements, rocking left and right.

"Here we go, Mom." I began to circle around the chair, gently holding my mother's hand in mine. Up over her head and around. When I had gone full circle, I let go of her hand, took hold of the wheelchair armrests, and began turning the chair.

"It's a waltz, Mom. One, two, three. One, two, three." I moved the chair in time to the music. "Forward two, three; back two, three. Forward two, three; back two, three." A slow turn again in front of her. Letting go of her hand, I bowed.

"Thank you for the dance, madam."

As I straightened up from my bow I saw my mother had dipped her head down, eyes closed in acknowledgment.

Mom rested her chin in her hand and looked off to the side. "I suppose we could dance for my birthday." She peeked at me without turning her head, like she was at the crossroads of a decision. Excited Mom was coming back.

"Yes, we will. We'll dance for everyone."

Mom contemplated this with a thoughtful look down. A slow nod. "You pick the music."

I was doing the fist pump internally. *Yeeee-sss.* "Of course, madam. It will be my pleasure."

"And bring the biggest chocolate chip cookies you can find for the biddies." She had her pride.

"Yes, and a cake for you."

She shrugged, but smiled as she glanced away.

Now I was curious. "Do you remember how old you will be?"

Mom looked intrigued at this question. "How old?"

"Well, how old do you think?"

"Seventy?"

"Mom, you will be eighty-nine years old next Thursday."

My mother's face was a mosaic of emotions. She went from looking completely surprised, to wondering, and then absolutely delighted. Her dark brown eyes actually sparkled like I hadn't seen in weeks. She sat up straighter as a smile captured her face. "Really! I look pretty damn good."

"That you do, Mom. That you do."

LEAVE-TAKING

Blossom stories allow me to laugh at my actions because I've seen from others how the "lesson" actually works. Betty is a great storyteller and shared this over coffee at a diner. It blossomed even more with the addition of our couples club and my marriage. Neither Betty nor Hodges have high blood pressure, and they still hold hands when they go out together.

Betty and Hodges had been married for forty-one years, which made them icons in our couples support group. They had been the founders and facilitators of the group for fifteen years. By the time my husband and I joined, they were respected and beloved leaders. Hank and I were still in what we learned was the power struggle phase of our marriage. Since my first marriage had ended in the death of my husband, I wanted to replicate what was great in that marriage. Having his first marriage end in divorce after seventeen years, Hank wanted tabula rasa.

Most of us in the group were on second or third marriages. We averaged six to ten couples at a meeting. Some were moving into the serious stage of yet another live-in relationship. We were all at various periods of adjustment from blended families with the settling of boundaries and turf battles, to empty nest silences and bewilderment, to the tweaking of routine responsibilities. Our friend Buddy's latest marital ultimatum was, "I have taken out the trash once a week

148

for thirty years; that's one thousand five hundred and sixty times. It's time to renegotiate this."

Hank and I were almost smug the night we shared our rules for fighting fair. After almost two years of Hank's icy silences as an argument deflector followed by my high drama of crying and/or storming out of the room, we admitted exhausted defeat in our old ways of spousal conflict resolution. We now committed to open verbal communication and were learning "active listening" with each other.

I no longer grabbed the car keys and stormed out after he winged a sarcastic "Fine, I don't care" at me in the middle of an argument. We were becoming pros at "So what I hear you saying is you think three hundred dollars is a tad too much for a birthday present for a preschool grandchild."

We glided through "Yes, I love to do things with you. However, if we don't plan ahead, it won't happen." This was countered with "Yes, dear, I agree about planning ahead, *and*—" (*and*, not *but*) "—I am having difficulty planning activities in fifteen-minute time slots between your meetings and luncheons. How about we slot *our* activities first at the beginning of the week?"

We knew about avoiding "gunnysacking," that dramatic but emotionally costly weapon of saving up resentments and then dumping them out over one seemingly minor event.

Hank and I had also learned to choose times to discuss an issue so we were more likely to get a positive response. I did not greet him at the door at 6:30 PM after his two-hour commute with "What the heck happened with the recycling this morning?" He did not pose any questions to me when my hand was gripped around my first mug of coffee.

Most of us in the couples group had eliminated red-flag phrases like "You always..." or "You never..." from our disagreement conversations. We had added soothers like "I have a request," and the universal bridge over troubled waters, "Thank you."

Each Monday brought fresh examples of marriage and relationship hurdles from those brand new to the marital highway as well as those who, like Hank and me, had traveled this sometimes bumpy road before.

Hodges and Betty were childhood sweethearts, having marched shoulder to shoulder into marriage, kids, grandkids, and on into retirement. "Still married to the same person," someone always said to newcomers, nodding in the general direction of the Icons over coffee and cookies pre- or postmeeting. The newcomers would twist around to get a glimpse of this interpersonal phenomenon. Some Mondays the glimpse might be of Betty and Hodges arriving hand in hand, wearing their Sunrise Bowling jackets—he bowled, she sat and knitted while she watched.

Or they might hear Hodges' laugh as he slapped one of the men on the back, looking over his shoulder as he called, "Betty, come meet this fine young man."

Then it happened. Two Monday evenings in a row, Betty arrived at the meeting without Hodges. The first Monday, we all noticed and exchanged sidelong glances. Some of the newer members leaned to look in the hallway to see if Hodges was ambling in a bit late, having stopped to smile and hug his fans on the way in. After all, it's a bit of a walk to our basement meeting room at the local library. No Hodges. When he finally did arrive ten minutes later, we were relieved, but confused. Our lovebirds coming separately? They sat next to each other. Everything seemed okay, but...

At that next Monday meeting, everyone, I mean everyone, swiveled to look at Betty when she walked in sans Hodges. "We've decided to come in separate cars," stated Betty.

A deathly silence settled over the group. Eyes darted left and right. What's with this? Coming separately. Was there—A Problem?

"No. No problem," said Betty. "H. was complaining about waiting for me after the meeting was over. I like to stay and talk. He goes straight from here to home and *Dancing with the Stars*. He's never danced in his life but now claims to know the nuances and differences between fox trot and quickstep, waltz and Viennese waltz.

He even drops dance names like Argentine Tango and Paso Doble into conversations." Her voice mixed with a chuckle, although her eyes did squint a bit as she added, "And he's now an expert on the female dancers' costumes."

"Okay, okay," we murmured. But I was thinking, *Is she giving us some flimsy cover-up for deeper issues? No, no, that's not Betty's style. It's probably just as she says.*

Betty summed up, "The show starts at 9:00 PM, and I'm not willing to cut short my talk time after the meeting. I told Hodges, rather snippily I admit, 'Hey, if it's so important to be home at 9:01, take the other car to the meeting, and then you can leave without me.' He called my bluff and, surprisingly, we found it works for us."

Some of us sighed. This made sense. I myself embraced the idea wholeheartedly. I remembered the first time my husband and I were at a social event together. We had MapQuested how to get to the party. We had planned an emergency signal if one of us got stuck with a boring talker. We had *not* discussed leave-taking.

Around 10:30 of party night my husband said to me, "You know, I'll be ready to go soon."

"Okey doke," I replied, digging into the homemade cheesecake and looking around for a final cup of coffee.

Next thing I knew, my sweetie had transported himself to the front door, had his jacket on, was holding my coat, and had started jiggling the car keys. I had just begun the process of saying good-bye to my dear friends, which cannot be accomplished with a "See you" to the group at large. It must be done one to one. And the hostess must get a special thank you, hug, kiss, and adieu.

Soon. He had said soon. This is when I had my first on-site learning experience of what "soon" meant for Hank. "Soon" meant "now."

After twenty-four years of marriage, "soon" continues to mean "now."

As in, "Hank, when do you want to eat?"

"Soon." These days, I know to get up within the next two minutes and move to the kitchen where he has already opened the refrigerator door and is doing that up and down bob and weave to check the offerings on the shelves.

Subsequently I learned when Hank actually said "now" in connection with a leave-taking, it meant he was extremely uncomfortable and I must pare good-byes to the hostess only, and we had to immediately move as one to the door and exit. This would require a later debriefing as to what caused the missing of the "soon" stage and what escalated it to "now." Hank is not manipulative, and I accept that my other good-byes will be accomplished later by phone.

There was some tension that first Soon Night on the way home. We did have WIC (Words in Car). Not a fight, but a fairly strong disagreement. We sifted through the decades of relationship routines, both of us determined to be right. We finally agreed to set an estimated time of departure (ETD) before future dates. This works for approximating when we will leave the party to come home.

ETD has also recently been utilized in leaving the house at the beginning of the evening. "When do you want to leave to go to the restaurant?"

"Soon." Uh-oh. Too vague.

With an ETD from home, Hank and I are assured that any tension will be reduced. It eliminates the need for my dressed and ready-to-go sweetie to inquire, "Are you ready yet?" as he appears in the bathroom doorway. This doorway question used to occur just as I was about to apply mascara to my pitifully thin lashes, always causing a startle reflex resulting in black dots under my lower lid, which delayed the actual departure time.

Given the remnants of leave-taking confusion and difference in social needs that my husband and I still experience, I envision departures of a smoother variety. Lately I find I kind of like the presence of Hank's ever-ready personality as I dash to get my purse, check that I turned off the curling iron, and then back to the purse for a phone, glasses, and keys check. Hank is bemused; I am laughing. We'll get there.

Somewhere along the spectrum of his "soon" and my "soon" is

"shortly." Hank uses "shortly" when he wants to do something in less than a half-hour. This dovetails almost perfectly with my "soon."

Hank: I'm ready to go soon.

Me: How about if we go shortly?

Hank: Okay.

And we both arrive at the exit of party, store, or garage door at the same time. It's amazing.

However, the Betty and Hodges separate car arrangement appealed to me for those times when either my beloved or I have shorter wait time or negotiation tolerance.

At our last couples meeting, I cornered Betty. "Betty, does it really work? Is there no animosity as to one of you wanting to get your way? How much later do you arrive home?"

"If we don't have far to go, it's a perfect setup," she replied. Ticking off on her fingers, "One, I don't have to feel guilty watching him do the hotfoot dance by the door. Two, we both are still given to offer unsolicited driving tips even after all these years together. So separate cars eliminates that particular irritation. Three, sometimes I'm a half-hour later, sometimes fifteen minutes."

She took a deep breath and squeezed my arm, her eyes gleaming. "But the best is my arrival home. I hear the ballroom music at full blast. There is a little tray of cheese and crackers on the coffee table. The teapot is on the TV tray table. I see Hodges sitting in his favorite chair, smack in front of the TV, remote in hand, and ... fast asleep."

OUR ANNIVERSARY

A full story as I looked back over twenty-four years of marriage. What's in your garden of anniversaries?

The seeds for my love of books were planted in childhood. I grew up feeling as if I personally knew the Bobbsey twins, Nancy Drew, and Trixie Belden. Wherever I have lived, I had a new library card within two weeks of moving. As an adult I read *Gone with the Wind* each winter, and have agonized over Cathy and Heathcliff"s lost love in *Wuthering Heights* at least four times.

But there is one book I have read twenty-four times and each time it is filled with new meaning. It is the book of wedding vows that my husband and I compiled when we got married on October 21,1989. It went through several rough drafts and rewrites. We first read it to each other from folded and refolded yellow legal pad papers. We next read it to each other in front of the guests at our wedding ceremony in my sister's living room.

When our first anniversary approached, my gift to my husband was a handwritten book of the ceremony bound together in a folder tied with ribbon and placed on the dining room table. "Let's read it to each other as if it were our wedding day, even though it's just the two of us."

After some discussion, we even removed our wedding rings for the exchange part of our vows. As we read it aloud, I was so emotion-

154

ally moved that tears came to my eyes. I felt the same joy and pride of our wedding day when we first publicly declared our love in front of our families and God. We looked at our small book of wedding photos and did a lot of "remember when" from that day.

Each year since, my husband and I have repeated this renewal ritual. We now sit by our lovely fireplace and light candles for the anniversary evening reading. We have two cut crystal glasses that we fill with sparkling cider. We take off our rings and place them by the handwritten book. We take turns reading our vows to each other. The exchange of rings is still the most poignant for me. My hands are now speckled with age spots; I no longer wear red nail polish. This last year, my ring protested as I slid it over the knuckle of my ring finger swollen by arthritis.

Our "remember whens" include events of the year just past, and over the years—our blended family, the lines between his side of the family and mine becoming blurred with love and support. We have milestone events that we've shared—our grandson's birth; birthdays; graduations; retirement; our loving and caring about daughters, nieces and nephews, and siblings; and the passing of my parents and his sisters, my cousins, and more recently some of our own peers. We celebrate our move to Arizona, and give thanks for our health and friendships we have made here in the Southwest.

The joy and pride we feel each October renews our spirit and commitment to our marriage. For me, it is as if I were a new bride again.

CATHERINE THE GREAT

True, happily, all true! How grateful I am to have a friend like Catherine at the dentist's office.

I consider myself to be a courageous woman. I'm adventurous. I did assertiveness training, took karate, rappelled into a snake's nest. I've led intervention groups with teenagers. I am woman, hear me roar!

But my track record of courage has been marred biannually by the phone call and chirpy voice that says, "Good morning, Ethel, it's time to schedule your dental checkup." My teeth have betrayed me with their thin enamel and nerve sensitivity. I am a woman with teeth that would, if they could, retract into my gums like a turtle pulls its head inside its shell. I am woman, hear me whimper.

This has meant decades of being unable to smile at my friend's uncle simply because he decided to become a dentist. Watching and hearing my husband chew ice—well, I'd rather walk on hot coals. Over the years my sensitive teeth have led to more than one dentist backing away in horror from my screams, feebly defending themselves, "But I barely touched you."

However, my phobia and paranoia have been eradicated by the appearance of Catherine the Great. Catherine is my dental hygienist.

I started going to Wilmot Dental Center not only because the dentist was highly recommended and the location was conveniently near my house, but also because of Catherine, dental hygienist extraordinaire. She is a modest-looking woman with a flippy kind of hairstyle and lovely laugh lines bracketing her generous smile, which exposes fine, straight, white teeth.

Not California white. Vacationing in southern California, I was almost blinded by the glaring realization that everyone in our neighbor state on the coast has very white teeth, not just the thirty-somethings. Teenagers, seniors, even very old people have white teeth like headlights, dazzling you with their mega wattage. But I digress.

I get my teeth cleaned twice a year because I have finally learned that this is the better way. Avoidance led to cavities, and now in my middle age, it has manifested itself in cracked crowns, cavities under the crowns, and the bizarre personality changes wrought during root canal. So I brush, floss, and eat sliced, not whole, almonds. And go to the dentist.

Two days ago I heeded the call and went for an audience with Catherine.

Catherine the Great, dental hygienist extraordinaire, always pauses in the entryway when it is your turn to go into her inner sanctum. "You will be received now" is the message, but it is a benevolent reception, one stirring up memories of fairy godmothers and royal personages who embody wisdom, compassion, and a way with dental instruments. I feel soothing vibrations wafting over to me as I gather my purse, magazine, glasses, and ebbing courage.

A kindly-looking woman with three young children in tow presses her lucky rabbit's foot into my hand as I stagger past her. "Here, honey," she says, "you need this more than I do."

I barely know how I get to Catherine's little office, such is the level of my anxiety. Numbly I follow her straight and confident back to The Chair. I sit. She leans amiably against the counter as she draws on her lavender nonlatex gloves.

"How are things since I saw you last?" She doesn't mean my nocturnal grinding, flossing habits, or enamel content. She seems to really want to know what's new. By the time I have described my trip to San Diego, land of white dentifrices, she has me bibbed, suctioned, and the chair is slowly reclining. I resume breathing.

Catherine has already produced The Pick. Since I am such a chicken and have had nerve zaps from past dental events, there is no sonic cleaning tool for me. It's the old by-hand method, gentle in Catherine's hands. No stranger to The Pick and its mercurial ways, my body tenses, my eyes cross as it approaches, sweat glands I didn't know I had start producing. Light tap and tiny scratch on my upper bicuspid. Her hand gently touches the edge of my right shoulder. "This will not be long. So, what do you think of my new addition?"

Her office is an aquatic oasis in the midst of the desert. The floor-to-ceiling window in front of us offers a view of a small green miracle. Plants, grasses, and flowers line the window, creeping up and hanging down the entire length of the glass. My neck muscles start to release their lock on my shoulders. A hummingbird flits to the feeder in a scene straight out of *Sleeping Beauty*. The irrigation bill must be intense.

Catherine must also be a Pisces. Crystal, ceramic, glass, and paper mobiles of fish, shells, and mermaids hang from the ceiling like her royal attendants. This draws the eye of the patient upward when not staring straight into hers. How do dentists and dental hygienists deal with that? They seem to develop the ability to stare back without any other facial tics, like the little smirk usually exhibited when two people find themselves in an undeclared staring contest. Dentists have a kind of gaze rather than stare, and into upside-down faces too.

I look up and to the left. In between the strings of the blue fish mobile and the green glass seaweed mobile is a long delicate strand of dental floss. Swaying slightly at the end is a studded starfish made of what can only be diamonds. And why not diamonds? This is, after all, the office of Catherine the Great.

I sigh deeply. This woman, who I see but two times a year, is someone with whom I have forged a relationship of candor, humor, and trust. Not an easy thing in a dentist's office.

Catherine gently takes the shredded tissue I used to wipe off my lipstick, and now have decimated, and presses a fresh victim in my hand. "Let's get into those nooks and crannies." The Pick moves in again. "Mmm," she murmurs from behind her mask. "You have beautiful gums."

Now I have had various compliments over the decades that have done much to boost my ego and help garner a sense of well-being. But this one fortifies me. She likes my gums!

She continues. "Your gums will support these teeth for a lifetime." I have gums that will help me fight the battle of fear, of pain! I hear Helen Reddy singing again in the background! I am woman, hear me roar!

The Pick moves on. Upper right, front, upper left. Scratch. A tiny flicker of pain. She stops instantly. Her hand presses my shoulder. "Let's take a rinse." Another training tool that dental professionals use, the shared phrasing, almost convincing their patients they also share our pain and anxiety. Chair rises up. We pause for a rinse that refreshes.

We (she's got me doing it) descend back again. We're on the lower teeth now. "Ah," she says, leaning back slightly. But it's an "ah" that does not signal distress or a foreshadowing of dollar bills flying out of my bank account to finance a post and crown and the dentist's next Alaskan cruise. And here is the coup de grace.

"Some people would kill for your saliva glands." This does more to distract me from pain than any gas, Novocain, or musical playlist. "Huh?" I garble. "Wha'?"

"Yes, you have very active glands." The suction tube again dangles from my jaw. "This is a good thing. It will keep your mouth healthy. Not every one has glands like this." She shakes her head in what can only be massive admiration. "Okay, we're almost done."

Catherine the Great has conquered my fear for me. I am lost in the glory of this most unique compliment! People would kill, not for my thighs, skin, hair, or other nonexistent attributes. My most valuable genetic talent appears to be centered on my ability to spit.

KIND

Germinating from a small block of wood, growing into Hank's decision story, this blossomed into a reciprocal kindness story.

It's happening again. I am sure I have the best husband in the whole world. This is not a Stepford wife thing. I'm not a whatever-you-want-honey type of mate. In fact, I might be categorized as frank, honest, or direct.

But this husband of mine. He is extraordinarily agreeable. I mean it. Agreement upon solicitation:

Example 1: "Hank, do you think you could sweep off the patio some time this weekend?"

"Sure, I'll do it now."

Example 2: "Hank, my computer isn't backing up. Could you ... ?"

"Hold on, I'll be right there."

Or unsolicited agreeable:

Example: "Here, Eth, I brought you some coffee." He has, and it's just the way I like it. Equal amounts of half-and-half and coffee, two demitasse spoonfuls of turbinado sugar, stirred into a blue Starbucks mug.

It's not as if he doesn't have a life and is waiting for me to give him a honey-do list. He plays golf, goes on double-digit-mile hikes with other fanatics in the Catalina Mountains, and has long and laughing phone calls with his sister and elder daughter, both of whom are thousands of miles away. He reads voraciously, sees the tech world and Internet library connections as user friendly, and has a rich interior life that expresses itself in intelligent and objective thoughts about people, history, and life's purpose.

He is truly a person of great value to me.

I knew our United States national park system was considered a national treasure. My dad, whose favorite quote about the United States was, "It's a great country," often talked about the national treasures of Niagara Falls, Gettysburg, and Washington, DC. When I read that Brazil declared Pelé, the soccer star, a national treasure in 1962 after Brazil won the world soccer title, I had an aha moment.

Why shouldn't a person of great value be a national treasure too? I moved Hank from person of great value to the category of national treasure. Now when I tell my Hank anecdotes to friends, I add my recommendation that he be declared a national treasure.

Not that he is without his warts. But that is another story.

Back to my extolling the virtues of Hank, aka a national treasure. Part of me puts his agreeable behavior in the emotional container that holds All Needs Fulfilled for Ethel. Yes, this is self-centered. There are no promises here of total maturity despite my supporting therapists for many years of my adult life. What these exchanges stir up in me are: *He loves me. I am cherished by my husband.* Having spent many years reading romance novels, I can run with these thoughts like a nimble high school quarterback who just knows he's gonna make that touchdown. I am in a bubble of bliss with all this agreeableness wafting around the house. I build on this as more proof of our marriage vows. *Not only does he love me, he loves me BEST. I am beloved.*

This is all true, but then the mature part of me remembers the last time I got into this bliss bubble. It burst. I mean, bliss is okay and can even be a positive experience, but to drift along entirely inside the bliss bubble is to forget the world around you. This creates an isolated viewpoint and one that is gradually unbalanced. Like me trying to sustain the tree pose in yoga after weeks of not practicing. I'm gonna topple.

Several years ago, I had a moment of crystal-clear insight about a situation that had been developing in our home. My husband was acting differently. He wasn't jumping into gleeful gossip with me anymore. He did not include a list of grievances about certain coworkers when he came home from work. He was not berating the TV commentators on the nightly news. He was being...so kind. The quota for verbal "I love yous" from him had gone up—daily.

That was about the time he started bringing me coffee when I was writing in my office. Not bringing it upstairs and then asking me to make some copies for him or type something, or more innocuous, but still an interruption, sitting and talking pleasantly. Just bringing me coffee and leaving the room. How kind!

This went on for days. *Wow, this is cool.* I was basking. I was floating in this kindness like a kid in a pool on a hot, sticky August day.

Example: I was taking my tote bags out to the car. It seems I can never, I mean never, go anywhere without a tote bag or two. Hank has been known to say, "Why can't you just be ready to leave the house and not have to dash around gathering up bags like an impulsive kid?" But this time he took them from me and put them in the trunk. *Clunk.*

"Ready to go?"

"Uh, yeah, I guess I am at that. Thanks."

Another example: I was going to visit my mother at the nursing home, which could be either a new pearl on the necklace of understanding she and I were stringing together, or it could be a gut-wrenching visit with her crying and lamenting being alone. As I gathered up keys and flowers and looked in my pockets for bits of compassion, he said, "Wait up. I'll go with you today."

"That is so kind of you."

"Mmm." He shrugged. "I lost my parents so many years ago. You're lucky you have a mother with you yet. Your mother has sort of become my mother. And it will help you to have another person there if this is a tough visit."

Several days after this, I was sitting at our breakfast table, which was in a nook of sunlight offering a view of the woods behind our house. Still basking, I had set the table—plates, napkins, juice, butter, and toast. Hank was finishing up the eggs. After he put my plate in front of me, he sat down with his.

I sighed. "I feel so loved. Thank you. You are so kind to me. I feel so special."

Hank smiled. He began his ritual of slicing into the sunny-side-up egg so the yolk opened, christening the white part and seeping over toward the toast. Then he looked at me and reached across to the middle of the table. Set among our salt and pepper shakers was a small block of wood.

"Remember this?" he asked.

He put the wooden piece in my hand. It was something I'd picked up years before after a holistic retreat. It was about one inch square, smooth, lacquered over a single word—KINDNESS.

"I decided to use this," he said.

"Oh, Hank, how wonderful. That's what I've felt lately."

He finished the egg prep, buttered the toast, and was into his first bite. "I've felt it too," he said. "I've been using it with my boss, with the staff at work, even on the train."

Ping! My little bliss bubble burst. "Oh, not just me." My voice sounded downright petulant. I started to laugh. "Here I thought I was so special. That you were spoiling me with kindness. Turns out you've got enough to go around."

"Huh? Well, I do love you best." And he bent over his plate again.

So here we are at least ten years later and I'm getting this bliss bubble feeling again. He is being so agreeable. But also I think my national treasure may have discovered another path to higher consciousness. Whatever it is I'm sure I'll find out. Meanwhile, I'll just bounce along in the bubble for a while. But first, let me pour this coffee for him into that brown ceramic mug that keeps it really hot, just the way he likes it.

LEAVE-TAKING II

Joanie would deny the length and circuitous route of this departure routine, but Ardin would nod his head knowingly. It all came together in one night as I watched the entire "dance."

My friends Joanie and Ardin have been married for a quarter of a century. So they have learned each other's needs as far as social interaction with other people. Joanie is very outgoing—everyone gets a hello hug. Over the years I have seen her small body emit equal amounts of friendship energy to her female friends, along with hulking new boyfriends of her daughters and now granddaughters.

Being a closet social anthropologist, I have watched Joanie and Ardin's arrival and leave-taking routines at dinners and parties with great interest. This routine has been honed to a fine and seamless dance of lead, follow, and acceptance. It never varies.

Imagine the latter hours of a party, folks talking in small groups, some gathered around the dessert table, men in the family room, women sitting in a semicircle, layers of conversation swirling around them. Some couples dancing in the hall. It's been a great party, and now it's starting to wind down.

Ardin begins the leave-taking dance. He nonverbally signals Joanie that he wants to go. He waggles his eyebrows. He jerks his head in the direction of the door. Joanie either disregards or truly does not see his gestures. The pros and cons of this kind of silent communication via body language is rich subject matter for another story, not to be debated here.

Next, Ardin is standing next to Joanie. He touches her elbow. "Joanie, we have to say good-night."

Joanie sweeps her eyes away from the conversation with a big smile. "Yes, Ardin. Okay."

Without missing a beat of this pas de deux, Ardin moves to get their coats. He is gone for several minutes. Joanie has not moved from her group. Ardin stations himself by the front door with coats and car keys. Two minutes pass. "Joanie. Joanie." A bit louder. "JOANIE!"

Joanie stands up, bends over to kiss each and every member of her little group. Her part of the dance commences. "Yes, Ardin, I'm coming."

This is where a tracking device would yield some fascinating data. Joanie physically moves into her leave-taking, first moving in the *opposite* direction from the front door so she can complete the full good-bye routine. Stopping at each group to kiss, say good-night, and often to take out her iPhone to make bridge, tennis, and lunch dates, she gradually makes a loop of the party area to the front door and her ride.

Ardin is as impassive as a ceremonial guard at Buckingham Palace. When Joanie is about halfway through her good-byes, he calls to her, "Joanie, I'll go get the car."

Joanie responds with a wink and a cheery "Okay, sweetie."

Ardin returns about six minutes later and resumes his post at the front door. Finally they merge and there is a fond farewell with the host and hostess.

"Come on, Joanie, let's go."

"Oh, Ardin, I'm coming." She hooks her arm through his into their closed dance position and looks up at him, smiling. "Wasn't it a lovely party?"

This is where I edge closer to catch the verbal exchange and narrow my eyes for a better look. Will he have a sarcastic remark about how long he has been waiting? Will he be silent, but signal displeasure merely by looking at his wristwatch?

He helps her on with her coat. "Yes, yes, but it's getting late." He stops for the finale of their dance as she faces him, and he slowly and tenderly slides his hand along the side of her cheek. "Let's go home."

WALKING THE LABYRINTH

*"The labyrinth is an ancient spiritual tool, a walking medita-
tion, a path of prayer. Walking the labyrinth can reduce stress,
quiet the mind, open the heart, and bring one closer to God.
People come to the labyrinth to heal, to be enriched in the
spiritual life, seeking peace, seeking insight."*
                                    —Sig Lonegren, *Labyrinths*

I walked the labyrinth this morning. I knew there was a labyrinth
at the Redemptorist Center in Tucson, Arizona, where I am for
a self-directed writing retreat. And I knew I'd make time to take
my walk.

My first labyrinth walk over twenty years ago at a Spring Hill,
Massachusetts retreat was filled with stops and starts, looking around,
feeling almost dizzy with the twists and turns. Now I look forward to
drifting along the path, not knowing how long or which turns will get
me to the center, but knowing I will get there.

When I woke up at 6:00 AM, my first thought was, *Ah...laby-
rinth.* As I left my room, I could see the eastern sky was bright behind
the splitting clouds. And yet a dark thought flickered like the floaters
that can come in your eye. *What if it's not there anymore?* My pace
quickened as if that was the guarantee that the faster I got to the labyrinth area, the more sure it would be to still exist.

❧

169

There's the open space around the bend. Good. Yes, it's there. It looked the same—flat dirt, rock-lined paths that I had walked before, with the small altar of rocks in the center. It's set back along a path near the petroglyph rocks and under the protective shadow of a small hill that is the location of the stations of the cross.

This labyrinth faces north, and the rainstorms of the day before seemed to be receding. Light in the east, but shadows still lurked behind the rocks. It was dim. Silent and serene.

Another sojourner is poised at the entrance or mouth of the maze, head bowed. I sit on the stone bench nearby and wait until she enters. I've never thought of a labyrinth as something you go through. You simply enter and move ahead, one step at a time.

A labyrinth is usually a flat layout in an open space—a life-size two-dimensional sacred maze along which to walk. The paths wind around and back and forth, leading to the center area.

Some people walk while repeating a mantra; some walk in silence; some use "empty mind." Some use it as a walking meditation, or a stream of consciousness walk.

I am entering this morning with an empty mind. But I hold the intention of keeping my head where my feet are. To drop the people and problems and to-do lists that I mentally packed along with my laptop, sneakers, and toothpaste. To stay in this moment.

I look north as I stand at the mouth of the labyrinth. The mountains are a grayish purple in the morning light. The cholla, prickly pear, and small saguaros around me are like sentinels watching in silent support. There is also a very green ground covering, which is unusual here in the Sonoran Desert. It rained last night, and everything is darkened and saturated to a deeper hue by the rain. Not a dull and heavy darkness, but a comforting velvety dark.

This labyrinth is in marked contrast to the one I walked at St. Mary's in San Francisco, which was a concrete-etched oasis in the midst of office buildings, and in the shadow of the old elegant Fairmont Hotel.

As I stand here, I become mindful of my most recent spiritual directive—to respond in a different way to people, places, and things. My goal is to build and hold a feeling of compassion for others and myself. I focus on the labyrinth's middle, where a pile of rocks rests at the epicenter of my walk. I visualize Compassion waiting to welcome me. In I go.

I say this intention several times: *May I respond in a different way to people, places, and things, leading me toward my goal of compassion for myself and others.* I look down as I walk. This desert labyrinth is laid out in the dirt and so has a reddish floor. The rocks that border the sides of the path are the sizes of different coffee mugs—some dainty, some the super size of a Starbucks mug. They are like the gray uniformed guards at the Chicago Art Museum, steady and silent but joining you in sharing information to guide you if you get lost. These rocks are gray, or spotted, some wearing little top hats of moss, reminding me of a labyrinth I walked at Cape Cod.

The smaller pebbles that cover the path crunch under my feet. I watch the toes of my blue sneakers as they peek out from the hem of my pants, taking me ahead. I am calm and peaceful. The March air is cool, almost cold, and the feeling on my cheeks reminds me of being outside in the snow.

Time recedes, but a thought intrudes. *Am I going the right way?* I've been walking for a bit of time, but the center still seems far away. I have to laugh because this happens every time I walk a labyrinth. *Have I stepped across a rock border to an earlier path? Did I get turned around? Am I heading out, missing the center entirely?* I stop and look back and into the center. *No. A labyrinth can be trusted. You will get to the center. You are exactly where you are supposed to be.* I have to remember this concept "out there" in the world when I think I've made an emotional, social, or mental misstep. I won't miss the plane, or meeting, or opportunity to make a new friend or forge a deeper relationship. I am going in the right direction and am exactly where I am supposed to be.

As my chuckle settles contently in my stomach, I look up to see the equivalent of spiritual nuns walking outside the labyrinth. Ten, maybe twelve women are walking single file, steadily heading straight toward me. Their spiritual garb consists of colorful shawls and long draped scarves wound around slender necks, UA sweatshirts, knitted caps on gray heads. Sneakers, hiking boots, and Uggs lead them on the curve around the hill toward the petroglyphs. They are so beautiful in their individual dress and uniform pace that I have to stop and stare as they file by until I can only see their retreating backs.

I resume walking. My fellow sojourner is moving at a slower pace, and I realize that I am going to be right behind her if I maintain my way of walking. I will be practically stepping on her heels. What to do? Is there labyrinth protocol for this? As I am flipping through my mental labyrinth etiquette files, she stops. *Oh no, is she going to do a midwalk prayer?* But as I get closer I realize she has moved five inches over a rock border and is motionless, waiting for me to go past. She must have felt me coming and moved over and then back after I passed for both her comfort and mine.

"Thank you," I murmur as I go past. She nods. *Remember this too, Ethel. Things work out without worry or angst and sometimes even without you having to orchestrate it. You can simply move on.*

When I look up again, there is the center. Compassion is there. Rock piled upon rock from a large flat one on up, smaller and smaller, making the two-foot-high natural altar. Meditators have left offerings on the top rocks. More than I have ever seen at a labyrinth. A wristband, a picture of Mary, other tiny rocks, a button that says *12 +12 =good math*, a paper clip!

I have nothing physical to place there. *What would I like to bring to such a sacred place? What do I want to leave there to be enveloped in compassion?*

The answer comes instantly. It is my brother-in-law, Paul. Paul, whose life was altered eight years ago by a stroke that forced part of his brain to go to sleep. Paul, who recently had a mini-stroke, bringing him another neurological storm of sorts that threw him off balance physically and emotionally. Paul, who got up every single day and showered, making himself look clean and handsome, and greeted me with "Hello hello! How is everybody today?"

I place my love for Paul on the top rock near the 12+12 offering. I am sure he would like that and also laugh to be in the company of a sacred paper clip.

I turn and begin the leaving. It's always quicker returning. Another truism to recall in the outside world.

More storms are predicted for this mid-March Saturday. Clouds are piling up over the northern mountains. But the sky is still slightly brighter in the east. Proof that there is always light, even if you can't see it.

The Garden: When a story comes in full blossom, as my experience did at the Redemptorist Center, I have to write it down immediately. I wrote the labyrinth story that afternoon. It was so easily remembered and cherished, needing very little in the way of details.

EPILOGUE

This last part is a bit preachy, well pretty much *all* preachy. But when I workshopped these last three pieces in various stages with different writers' groups, the comments were, "Wish I had this in my last marriage." "These are great!" "I could have saved myself a lot of angst if I had this." "Can I have a copy of this?" *Can you? You bet.*

I know this stuff works. I was the crazy chick in "Dysfunction Junction."

MAKING A LIST

Invitation to this part of the Garden: If you read self-help books, still believe in romance, and have decided you're ready to be honest with yourself...

If you remember a relationship that was based on potential rather than reality...

If you have had one sexy relationship after another and they each ended badly/poorly/sadly/violently...

It's time to do some brainstorm writing of your own. Now.

Make a relationship list. Write down what you want in an intimate relationship. Really want. Not what your sister has, not what your family wants for you.

What do the words *love, intimacy, trust, commitment,* and *honesty* mean? How does a person behave who has these qualities?

If you don't know what you want, write what you don't want.

If you have had lots of sexy partner relationships that don't last and your complaining drives your family crazy, do a timeline. Same if you have had multiple marriages or live-in relationships. What did you get from each? Be honest. Financial security, ego stroking, nurturing? What did you bring to it? Every relationship serves a purpose but perhaps is not the intimate relationship you know you want to have someday.

You might see you had the same relationship with a different face

177

and body. And the relationship probably lasted from one to three years. Aha moment. *That's why I felt so comfortable so quickly in each new relationship. It was déjà vu.*

Brainstorm means write without judgment or censure.

I had a list that grew after much, I repeat, much trial and error and R&D (research and development):

1. No married men. That expanded to include "I'm separated, but we haven't lived together for years."

2. No drugs. No drinking. No lying.

3. Employed with some financial security.

4. No new children on the horizon.

5. Has to be more of an adult than child in emotional development.

6. Good sense of humor.

7. Likes to read. Very verbal.

8. Somewhat physically active.

9. Has his own friends.

10. Physically affectionate.

11. Some idea of spirituality.

12. Also wants a committed, intimate, monogamous relationship.

Once you have your own list, decide honestly which of those things on the list you want and which you need. What is absolutely nonnegotiable on the list? What is negotiable? The list means the person you will consider having a relationship with will have these characteristics when you meet him or her, not the potential for them or be in the process of getting them. Throw out "But he has such potential" unless you are the therapist of the list maker.

Practice talking with people who have similar interests. Start with a superficial involvement. Try dating. Have your behavior match your list. If you want someone who doesn't drink, don't date people you meet at bars. Better yet, don't go to bars. If you want activity, join hiking groups. Hooray for Meetup! Eventually you'll want to be into one on one.

Move through what author Terri Gorski calls the levels of relationships, from acquaintance (Hi), to activity friend (We both like to hike), to companionship friend (We like the activity *and* each other), to intimate relationship (We're sharing our lists). Terri Gorski calls this a sexy friend.

Once in a relationship, acknowledge to each other, "Yes, this is an ongoing gig rather than a one-night stand."

Some couples acknowledge that they are "working" on their relationship. Too hard for me. I prefer "investing in this relationship." I like the idea of benefits and returns. And the benefits have proven to be far beyond my wildest dreams.

Occasionally my husband and I review our lists that brought us together. And we have added other activities to keep our relationship vibrant. Here are five possibilities to consider for a relationship review:

1. Make a new list. Write what you want in the relationship. Check it twice. Change your demands to requests.

2. Write down what first attracted you to your mate. Does it still?

3. What did you do in the beginning, in the early infatuation days? List those things. Do them.

4. What made you special to each other?

5. The Two-Question Update (with thanks to a Jack Canfield workshop in 1992).

First: "On a scale of one to ten, how would you rate our relationship?" Listen to the answer as objectively as possible.

Second question: If the rating is not a ten (come on, nobody's perfect), "What can I do to make it a ten?" Then pick one thing and do it.

Rules for Fighting Fair—It Can Be Done!

The Garden: After a couples weekend retreat, my husband and I came away with a framework for our rules list. I was already drafting our personal list on the drive home. If you identified even somewhat with "Dysfunction Junction" this rules piece may be a good one to keep.

"Be the architect of your new adult relationship, not the victim of an old one."

Here's where I briefly put on my family therapist hat, get an earnest look on my face, lean forward, and say, "Healthy, successful relationships contain basic negotiation knowledge."

If you want to have less tension in arguments in your relationship (personal, professional, organizational), terms like overall goal, personal goal, belief in win/win, trust building, piggybacking, brainstorming, active listening in communication, reaching closure, and affirming need to be vaguely familiar to the participants.

If this is all alien territory, do some reading, get a few face-to-face sessions in couples or family counseling, then definitely make some rules.

181

Some suggested rules follow. The alternative being you will probably approach arguments the *same* way and expect *different* results. You know that won't work.

1. Give yourselves permission to argue.

2. Know what you are fighting about. Be honest. Watch out for "surface" arguments.

3. Fight to reach a solution. Do you want to be happy or right?

4. Find one area of agreement. "Well, we sure are not getting along." "You got that right."

5. No gunnysacking. Gunnysacking is a seemingly innocent decision to save all hurts when they happen to avoid a fight, or to keep the peace. They are not discussed but put into an imaginary sack. But unfortunately you have kept the sack and then dumped it all out instead later when you just can't stand it anymore or it's used as retaliation to a criticism. Example: "You didn't pay the bill in December, and then you spent too much money in January. You didn't pick up the dry cleaning on Friday. Can't you do anything right?" The healthier alternative is taking just one issue at a time and working it out.

6. No name-calling or derogatory labels. "You're being hysterical" quickly serves to create a second argument or retaliation. "Well, you're indifferent to my feelings" distracts from the original problem because the name caller must now defend against the indifference accusation. It's a set-up for an emotional battle of wills. Exhausting too, right?

7. No aggressive physical contact. No hitting, pushing, kicking. No throwing of objects.

8. No crying.

9. No leaving without saying "I'll be back" or "I need time out."

10. No screaming. Talk low. Talk slow. And don't say much.

11. No mindreading. "I knew you'd do that. It drives me crazy."

12. Keep talking until you get on parallel roads.

13. Listen, then repeat what you think you heard the other person say.

14. No interrupting. Give wait time and silence while the other person formulates his or her answer.

15. Keep eye contact. No rolling of eyes, which is a silent way of demeaning others.

16. Model calm and acceptance.

17. Avoid using *always, never, everything, everyone.* "You are *always* late." Then the late person feels she has to find an example of when she was not late and you're off the subject of the disagreement. Do not let anyone deflect away from the topic of the argument. This deflection is sometimes called "creating brush fires."

18. Be aware of HALT. Are you hungry, angry, lonely, tired? If so, take a break; establish when you will talk again. "Let me calm down for ten minutes." Make sure you resume in ten minutes. Build credibility and trust in your relationship.

19. Use "I" statements. "I want to talk about something important. Can we do this tonight?" And use "When you_____, I feel _____."

20. Avoid "You should ... You have to ... You need to understand that ..." People don't really have to do anything. Instead try "It might help if you could ..." "If we are going to resolve this, I think we need to ..."

Add/delete/write your own rules.

THE ABCS OF RETIREMENT

The Garden: For several years I presented "The ABCs of Retirement" with a retired hairdresser named Al. He was in his seventies; I was in my fifties. He had retired due to chronic carpel tunnel syndrome. I had retired from teaching by choice. We were both extremely content, very active, and happy in retirement. We actually made ABC lists with participants at the workshops and had a lot of fun. Little did I know I would be revising and using this list several times more. Thanks, Al!

Two words express how I feel about my retirement days—*Ah, life!*

It's 1:30 PM. During my teaching career, at 1:30 I was simultaneously teaching a math lesson, helping a child understand the difference between nickels and quarters, writing out a contract for an independent reader, and surrounded by twenty-five second-graders. Mentally I was probably thinking of a 3:15 conference with a parent, wondering when I was going to write my lesson plans, and if I'd have a chance to just sit for a half-hour any time in the near future.

Today I'm at our local gym, or at the pool, or meeting with my writing partner, or traveling. Sometime during the day, my husband or I may ask, "Is today Tuesday?" "How did I ever get everything done when I was working nine to five?" (or eight to six, as the case may be), or "Did you ever think life would be this great?"

Don't get me wrong. I loved teaching. I was a cheerleader for public education. Today I am still a public advocate for the respectful education of children. But after twenty-eight years of working with young children I wanted, no, yearned for, a change. There is so much more to life. I wanted to work with adults, travel, and be with my husband and family in a more relaxed setting.

My transition in 1997 was a chosen one, a planned time (after twenty-eight years at the same school, and at age fifty), a semi-retired career (coaching and public speaking), and place for retirement (living in New Jersey until my husband retired, at which time we would make the cross-country trip to Tucson, Arizona, to begin our retirement life). Some people transition to retirement due to life circumstances, an illness, a downsize, a family obligation. We may have different perspectives, but we all have the same goal—a successful transition and a certain "they lived happily ever after."

For my transition, I turned to two sources. People and books. I read articles about how the baby boomers were going to change the definition of retirement. But my parents retired to North Carolina in 1975 when they were in their mid-fifties and enjoyed almost thirty years of good health as they traveled, square danced at concerts along the Atlantic Coast, and pursued their own interests. One of my teaching colleagues retired about ten years before I did. She and her husband were what I called Elderhostel groupies—they have traveled all over the world. Those folks were not baby boomers.

Retirement in our culture, as a new beginning, not just the end of working, has been going on for more than three decades. Research shows people are living healthier, happier, and smarter. The definition of what old is has changed. Today you are considered young up to age thirty. You are middle-aged from thirty to fifty. The young-old category is age fifty to seventy, and older people are in their seventies. The category of old-old is age seventy-five and up. I ascribe to the definition of old being what *you* decide.

I talked with people who had retired and seemed happy and successful. I spent time with people who had gone where I had not gone before. I picked their brains to learn their ideas, their plans. I read books. Then I got a spiral notebook and started brainstorming and writing down my dreams, my values, my reality, my timeline, and my goal.

I wrote a specific goal: *By June 1997 I will be retired from teaching and have a counseling office in Verona, New Jersey, and work part-time counseling, giving workshops, and writing, and get paid for the services I provide. I will visit Paris with my husband before the year 2000.* And it happened!

After accomplishing my 1997 goal I began setting new ones. And learned to be more specific in my goal statement. When I turned fifty, I started lessons in tae kwon do. At the urging of my instructor, I signed up for a competition in the kata forms (a series of memorized moves in karate).

Sensei (teacher): What is your goal for this tournament?

Me: To bring back a gold medal for our school, sir.

I was good in the competition and, yes, I did earn the gold medal. However, the other small bit of information was that I was the only person in my age category. So, drum roll please, I got the gold! I like to think I earned that gold medal, not just because I was the only senior in my category. But from then on I remembered Jack Canfield's recommendation for goal setting: Be very specific. Tell what, where, who, how, when, and why.

I used this "retirement" planning and goal setting again in 2004 when I officially closed my coaching business and began writing full time. My husband and I wrote our joint retirement goal in planning our move to Tucson in 2009.

As I read, talked, and observed people, I noticed the ones who were retired successfully (by that I mean they were secure, generally healthy, and not living with angst or drama) had common characteristics, hence the Post-It on my refrigerator: The Three As. They were Active, had a great Attitude, and had a basically affectionate Acceptance of themselves, other people, and life.

Research shows a happy retirement is not so much leaving something, but moving emotionally, physically, socially, intellectually, or professionally toward something else.

Since becoming a cheerleader for happy retirement, I am always on the lookout for positive retirement ideas. Here are two recent ones: AARP ad: "As you've proven with your lifestyle, being retired doesn't mean that you're tired." Del Webb's Sun Cities ad: "Retire from work. Not from life."

More and more articles and books talk about the ways in which the brain can rebuild learning pathways. This is known as neuroplasticity. I saw this with my brother-in-law actually relearning how to speak after a stroke.

Cognitive learning can be increased. AARP tells me to take up a new hobby. Join the Sudoku craze. Memorize new dance steps. You *can* teach an old dog new tricks. I regularly do the word games on Luminosity to keep my neurons limber.

I read that nouns are the first to go. Being a loving wife, I pointed this out to my husband when he seemed to be having extra-long pauses in recalling names. "You know, there are exercises you can do for that lapse." He ignored me, giving more credence to the adage "You cannot be a prophet in your own backyard." But he does remind me to do my own noun exercises when I stumble on my writing partner's last name or that thingy that holds our computer back-ups.

My new role models are not thin, or overly athletic, or necessarily billionaires. Some became famous in their second or third career, or their fifth, sixth, and seventh decade of life. A seventy-six-year-old woman had stopped embroidery because of arthritis and took up painting. She had the unassuming name of Grandma Moses. John Houseman was seventy when he starred in *The Paper Chase* series on TV. A grandmother became prime minister of Israel. Maggie Smith, Helen Mirren, Ruth Bader Ginsberg, all beautiful and accomplished. Today being a centarian is not unusual. George Burns lived to be a hundred.

What fills my life today is more than the three As of Attitude, Activity, and Acceptance. In fact, it's a whole alphabet. Being an ex-teacher, I couldn't resist the opportunity to include an ABC chart for readers.

When my mother was eighty-one, words that came to mind when I heard about her latest escapades were *feisty, laughing, verbal, wacky,* and *curious.* My brother-in-law got his pilot's license at fifty-five. He was determined. I published my first book at sixty—YES!

Roget's Thesaurus says to succeed is to flourish. *Well, that's okay.* To do well. *Hmm, very nice.* To be on top of the world. *Yes!* To be on the crest of a wave. *Ah!* What puts you on top of the world? What are your ABCs?

My ABCs of Retirement

A - Activity

B - Balance

C - Compassion, Commitment

D - Dancing

E - Energy

F - Family, Fidelity

G - Groups

H - Health, Hank, Humor

I - Investments

J - Journey

K - Kissing, Kindness

L - Love, Laughter

M - Marriage, Meditation

N - New things

O - Open to new ideas

P - Play

Q - Quirky

R - Relaxation

S - Spirituality, Security—financial, emotional

T - Travel, Toastmasters

U - Understanding

V - Vitality

W - Wisdom, Writing

X - Setting a happy eXample

Y - You

Z - Zest

Your ABCs of Retirement

A -

B -

C -

D -

E -

F -

G -

H -

I -

J -

K -

L -

M -

N -

O -

P -

Q -

R -

S -

T -

U -

V -

W -

X -

Y -

Z -

About the Author

E thel Lee-Miller, a native of Long Island, New York, is a retired teacher and now writer and public speaker with over three decades of educational and counseling experience. A transplant to Tucson, Arizona in 2009, she resumed her love affair with words through personal essays that explore the dances of relationships where love, adventures, indifference, dreams deferred, and joy are choreographed and performed.

Her first book, *Thinking of Miller Place: A Memoir of Summer Comfort* (iUniverse 2007), explores the joy of being an identical twin and a nostalgic look back at childhood in the 1950s.

Since moving to Tucson, Ethel has been active in the Society for Southwestern Authors and local writing groups. She is an International Women's Writing Guild Arizona representative and continues her membership in Toastmasters International. She also keeps in contact with her favorite New Jersey writing groups—The Write Group of Montclair, Scriveners, and Women Who Write.

Seedlings: Stories of Relationships is her second book. Relationship topic talks such as Making a List, Remarriage, Who's the Boss?, Fighting Fair, and Celebrating Love are parts of group book talk discussions with Ethel.

Editing services include copy, proofreading, and developmental editing. Writing workshops cover topics such as The Writing Process, Memories into Memoir—Getting Started, Memories into Memoir II, Marketing Your Book on a Shoestring, Creative?—Sure You Are!, and Public Speaking Without Panic for Authors.

To learn more about purchasing *Thinking of Miller Place*, workshops, and *Seedlings*, visit Ethel at:

eccheleemiller.com

etheleemiller.com

facebook.com/etheleemillerauthor

ADVANCE PRAISE

A provocative look at the precious people who share our lives, including a mother who dances at 89, a queenly dental hygienist, and a second husband who serves the heel of the bread. Read, enjoy, and inwardly inventory your own treasures.

—Lorraine Ash,
Author of *Self and Soul: On Creating a Meaningful Life*

Beautiful, fun, spirited stories on humanity and connection. Ethel writes with such grace and passion. Her stories will melt your heart. A fantastic read for all ages coming from all walks of life.

—Tara Kligman,
Holistic Health Coach, Bangkok, Thailand

"More alike than different" sums up this delightful collection. Ethel's fine eye for detail is matched by her ability to discover the common threads between us all, and to illustrate them touchingly, poignantly, and yet lightly in this, her best book to date. Each story is a window into the process of our lives. I can't wait to see what flows next from her pen—as a gift from her deep well of insight and compassion.

—Beth Lane,
Author of *Lies Told Under Oath*

Seedlings, a collection of personal essays and memoirs, exposes universal truths about the experience of being human with stunning simplicity. Ethel Lee-Miller cleverly uses her brilliant analogy of life's garden, with its seeds, shoots, and blossoms, to capture poignant moments and events in her life. The stories and characters are drawn so beautifully that any reader will readily identify with them. Be prepared to be moved to tears and laughter as she makes personal relationships assume an almost spiritual quality. *Seedlings* easily could be a life-changing book.

—Duke Southard,
Author of *A Favor Returned* and *Agent for Justice*

Seedlings is a gem—a work that starts out small and grows with each subsequent story. Ethel Lee-Miller has a gift for painting a picture with words and drawing the reader into her world.

—Janet M. Neal,
Author of *Soul in Control: Reflections of a Reformed Superwoman* &
Queen Bee at the Superbwoman™, Inc.

*Seedling*s is a collection of well-crafted essays that intertwine heart and humor with a bouquet of colorful characters. Honest and revealing sensory details translate Ethel Lee-Miller's personal stories to the reader's universal experience. A truly enjoyable read!

—Bridget Magee,
Writer, Poet, Speaker, Mom

CPSIA information can be obtained at www.ICGtesting.com
Printed in the USA
BVOW03s0801050514

352122BV00003B/14/P